William Harrison Ainsworth

The Spanish Match or Charles Stuart at Madrid

Vol. 1

William Harrison Ainsworth

The Spanish Match or Charles Stuart at Madrid
Vol. 1

ISBN/EAN: 9783337429454

Printed in Europe, USA, Canada, Australia, Japan

Cover: Foto ©Andreas Hilbeck / pixelio.de

More available books at **www.hansebooks.com**

THE
SPANISH MATCH

OR

CHARLES STUART AT MADRID.

BY

WILLIAM HARRISON AINSWORTH.

Carlos Estuardo soy,
  Que, siendo amor mi guia,
Al cielo de Espana voy
Por ver my estrella Maria.

LOPE DE VEGA.

IN THREE VOLUMES.

VOL. I.

LONDON:
CHAPMAN AND HALL, 193, PICCADILLY.
1865.

INSCRIBED

TO

JAMES BEAZLEY, Esq.,

OF

LIVERPOOL,

BY HIS MUCH OBLIGED FRIEND,

THE AUTHOR.

CONTENTS OF VOL. I.

BOOK I.

THE JOURNEY OF JACK AND TOM SMITH TO MADRID.

PAGE

XII.

How Jack and Tom witnessed a grand Ballet at the Louvre; and how Tom danced a Saraband with Anne of Austria, and Jack danced the Pavane with the Princess Henriette Marie . 169

XIII.

XIV.

XV.

XVI.

XVII.

The Spanish Match.

BOOK I.

THE JOURNEY OF JACK AND TOM SMITH TO MADRID.

I.

ON Monday, the 17th of February, in the year 1623, King James I. was alone in his private cabinet in the palace of Whitehall, engaged in perusing a despatch, which he had just received from the Earl of Bristol, then ambassador-extraordinary to the court of Madrid.

With the appearance of the monarch the reader must be familiar, so it is scarcely necessary to describe him, but we may mention, that on this occasion, as on most others, he was cased in a black silk doublet, so thickly padded as to be proof

B 2

against stroke of sword or dagger. This bolstered doublet gave him an air of excessive and unnatural corpulency, though in reality his frame was very meagre, as was shown by his legs, while his huge bombasted trunk-hose greatly impeded his movements and increased the natural ungainliness of his figure. There were more marks of age and decrepitude about James than were warranted by his years—he was then only fifty-seven—his cheeks were hollow, his eyes blear, his limbs shrunken, and he tottered in his gait like a feeble old man. His whole appearance, indeed, betokened that he was well-nigh worn out, and such was the opinion entertained of him by the courtiers, who, feeling assured he could not last long, had already begun to pay their devotions to the rising sun.

The intelligence conveyed to the king was evidently far from agreeable to him. Not only did he manifest considerable irritation, as by the aid of a powerful pair of glasses he got through the despatch, but at last he threw it down with an oath

—the British Solomon, as is well known, swore lustily when angered—and exclaimed, " By my saul! I will no longer be trifled with. The King of Spain is playing me false. I will break off the marriage-treaty at once, and recal Bristol." He then seized a pen, and adjusting his spectacles, began to indite a letter to the ambassador, in which he gave full vent to his displeasure, by no means mincing his phrases, but setting down whatever came uppermost.

While he was thus occupied, the door was opened, and two persons entered the cabinet. As they were unannounced by the gentleman-usher, James, among whose many infirmities deafness was numbered, did not hear them come in, and his back being towards the door, he did not remark their presence. So he continued his task, under the impression that he was alone, concocting his sentences aloud, and thus acquainting those near him with the secrets of his despatch, as well as diverting them by the coarse energy of his expressions. The foremost of the two would have interrupted him, but was checked by his companion, who whispered in his ear, "Let him alone. He will never send off that despatch."

The individual to whom these words were addressed, was a young man about two-and-twenty, whose noble lineaments and dignified deportment proclaimed him of the highest rank. In fact, he looked infinitely more like a king than the old monarch near whom he stood. His features were characterised by a gravity far beyond his years, and a shade of melancholy sat upon his brow, heightening the interest inspired by his handsome and thoughtful countenance. His eyes were large and black, his forehead lofty and capacious, denoting the possession of a powerful intellect, while his looks breathed taste and refinement. Moustaches and a pointed beard harmonised well with his somewhat lengthy visage, and his dark locks, divided above the temples, fell down in ringlets upon the starched lace ruff encircling his throat, and which served as a frame to his comely head—a head, once seen, never to be forgotten. His complexion was pale, inclining to swarthiness—a hue of skin supposed to belong to one of saturnine temperament. He was about the middle height, but held himself so erect that he seemed taller than he was in reality. His figure was slender, but perfectly proportioned, and his demeanour, as we have intimated, full of grace and majesty. His habiliments were of white velvet, and became him well, the doublet and hose being puffed with azure silk, and the mantle lined with the same stuff. His sole ornament was the diamond star upon his cloak.

In this striking-looking personage there will be little difficulty, we apprehend, in recognising Charles Prince of Wales.

The prince's companion was likewise very handsome—handsomer, indeed, than the prince—but he lacked the dignity of manner and singularly high-bred look that distinguished Charles. He was in the prime of manhood, being the prince's senior by about eight or nine years, and possessed a figure of unequalled symmetry. Well-favoured, however, as he was in form and feature, his haughty manner marred the effect of his good looks. His magnificent person needed no embellishment, yet his attire was splendid, his pink satin doublet and hose being covered with gems, while chains of large orient pearls hung from his neck down to his very girdle, which was likewise encrusted with precious stones. To the extraordinary personal advantages we have described, George Villiers, Marquis of Buckingham—for he it was—added great accomplishments, mental as well as bodily. Clear-sighted, keen-witted, eloquent, and if not learned or profound, he had art enough to hide his deficiencies. He was expert in all manly exercises; rode better than any one at court, won all the prizes at the tilt-yard, and danced more gracefully than Sir Walter Raleigh.

Seven years ago, on his first appearance at court, where he was introduced as a rival to the then reigning favourite, Carr, Earl of Somerset, young Villiers's remarkable graces of person and captivating manner at once attracted the king's notice, and his rise was incredibly rapid. Favours were lavished upon him by the infatuated monarch; he was ennobled, and eventually raised to the highest posts in the state. To enumerate all the important offices with which he had been gratified by his doting master would be tedious, but it may be mentioned, in order to give an idea of his power and greatness at the period in question, that he was Lord High Admiral of England, Lord Warden of the Cinque Ports, Constable of the Castle of Dover and of the royal Castle of Windsor, Lord President of the Council of War, Knight of the Garter, and first minister. Besides all these and many other posts and honours, he had a dukedom in expectancy.

Since his aggrandisement, however, Buckingham's character had materially changed. Affable at first to all, he had become excessively haughty and domineering, being insolent even to his royal master. Boundlessly profuse in expenditure, and insatiate, he well-nigh drained James's coffers. His entertainments were superb, surpassing in splendour those of the king. His retinue was that of a prince; his carriage was drawn by six horses, and if he rode forth a large escort attended him. No wonder that his insufferable arrogance and imperious deportment alienated his partisans and increased the number of his enemies—no wonder that his overthrow was frequently attempted. In vain. Buckingham proved too strong for his enemies. Favourite alike of father and son, of the king and the heir to the throne, he derided all opposition.

That Buckingham should have succeeded in ingratiating himself with a prince so grave and reserved in manner as Charles, whose character was so opposite to his own, and who was so likely to be distrustful of his advances, shows wonderful adroitness on his part, and proves incontestably that he possessed in the highest degree the art of pleasing. In order, however, to confirm his influence with the prince, he conceived a bold and singular project, to explain which a brief retrospect will be necessary.

James had long cherished the design of forming a matrimonial alliance for his son with Spain, and had made a formal proposition to Philip III. for the hand of his second daughter, the Infanta Maria; but though the offer was graciously received, and negotiations entered into, innumerable delays occurred, and his patience being at length exhausted by the dilatory Spanish cabinet, James put an end to the treaty. But though baffled, and offended by the duplicity which he supposed had been practised towards him, James had not altogether abandoned his design, and other circumstances occurring at a later period to render an alliance with Spain more than ever desirable in his eyes, he determined to renew his offer to Philip IV., who had just succeeded his father. In this matrimonial scheme, Charles, the principal person concerned in it, entirely acquiesced. Though he had never beheld the Infanta, the ravishing description he had received of her charms inflamed his breast with the strongest passion.

Accordingly, John Digby, Earl of Bristol, a diplomatist of approved ability, and who stood deservedly high in James's favour, was despatched as ambassador-extraordinary to Madrid to propose the match to Philip IV. The young king seemed far more favourably inclined to the alliance than his father had been, and declared that if the religious difficulties in the way of the union could be adjusted, all other points might be easily settled. But these difficulties were not easily removed. Months flew by—and the negotiation made little progress. As a preliminary measure, a dispensation had to be obtained from the Pope, Gregory XV., but this was refused unless the King of England engaged to mitigate the severe laws then in force against his Roman Catholic subjects. To this demand James assented, and began at once to carry his promise into effect. His ready compliance, however, induced the Pope to make further demands, and James was compelled to make additional concessions. Still the dispensation was delayed.

Things were in this state when the Conde de Gondomar, for many years ambassador to England, but who had recently returned to his own court, in order, if possible, to expedite the negotiation, wrote privately to Buckingham that he did not believe the match would ever take place, unless the prince came to Madrid to fetch his bride. "Bring him here," concluded Gondomar, "and the affair will be speedily settled."

The hint was not lost upon Buckingham. Persuaded that success would attend the proposed expedition, in which case the entire credit of accomplishing the union would attach to himself instead of to the Earl of Bristol, whom he hated as a rival, while the prince must needs feel grateful to him for procuring him a consort, Buckingham proposed the journey to Charles, assuring him that it was the only means of accomplishing the object he had in view, and offered to accompany him.

Fired by the romantic nature of the project, which exactly suited his character, Charles at once agreed to the proposition, thanked Buckingham for his zeal, and manifested the utmost impatience to set forth upon the journey.

The grand difficulty was to obtain the king's consent. His majesty was sure to raise numerous objections to the expedition, but these Buckingham undertook to remove. The prince's impatience would not brook delay, so, after arranging a plan of action, they entered the cabinet as described on the morning in question, resolved to carry their point.

They came at the very nick of time, since James, in his present mood, might have broken the marriage-treaty, and so have effectually frustrated their design.

For a few minutes after their entrance, the king continued his despatch, reciting aloud what he was setting down. He then paused, and while he was reflecting, Charles, advancing towards his chair, made a reverence, and said, "When your majesty is at leisure I crave a word with you."

"Bide awee, Babie Charlie—bide awee!" exclaimed the king. "I'm engaged on yer ain business—that confounded alliance with Spain, which has given me more trouble than aught I ever undertook. But I'll make an end of it now. Ha! is that you, Steenie?" he added, noticing the favourite. "Saul o' my body, lads, I canna say that ye are either of you welcome to yer auld dad at this moment, for he has been sairly put out by a despatch just received from Bristol—fresh delays— new demands — enough to drive one stark mad. You maun gie up all thoughts of the Infanta, Babie Charlie, for she never can be yours. I am about to break off the match."

"Not so, sire—not so!" cried his son.

"But I say 'yea,'" vociferated James, testily. "Hear what I hae written to Bristol, and then ye'll understand whether I'm in earnest or no."

"Your majesty need not trouble yourself to read the despatch," remarked Buckingham. "We know what it contains. But in spite of all that has happened—in spite of the dissimulation and perfidy of Olivarez—in spite of Bristol's mismanagement—in spite of the Pope—the match *will* take place."

"Ye are wrang, Steenie—ye are wrang," cried James. "I tell ye, man, I am about to break it off."

"Would you undo your own work, just when it is on the eve of accomplishment?" said Buckingham. "You are far too sagacious for that."

"Uds death! man, there's nae help for it," returned James. "I will mak nae mair concessions to please the Pope or the great Dule himsel, wha eggs him on. I hae made ower mony already."

"I should be the last to counsel your majesty to truckle to Rome," said Buckingham. "But you may dispense with the dispensation. I will stake my head that the match shall take place— ay, and before the end of April."

"Ye are a bauld man, Steenie—a verra bauld man," said James, laughing, "and can do maist things weel, but ye canna perform impossibilities."

"I can do what Bristol has failed to do, at all events," rejoined Buckingham. "And this is no idle boast, as your majesty will find, if you put me to the test."

"Ye say that safely, for ye ken fu' weel that I am not likely sae to try ye," observed James. "But let me make an end of my despatch."

At a sign from Buckingham, Charles then drew nearer to his father, and said, in an earnest voice, "I have a matter of importance to lay before your majesty, on which I desire to have your advice. But, before proceeding, I must have your royal word that you will not divulge the secret I am about to impart to any one—not even to your council. Otherwise, my lips will remain sealed."

"I hae nae secrets, as ye ken, frae Steenie," replied James, whose curiosity was aroused. " But sin' he is present, and will hear the secret—if he be not acquainted wi' it already, as I shrewdly suspect —there is na need to make an exception in his favour. Speak without fear, my bairn. I solemnly pledge you my royal word that I will keep your secret as close as I ought to keep my purse."

" Since I am thus encouraged," said Charles, " I can no longer hesitate to prefer my request. Gracious sovereign and father," he continued, prostrating himself before him, " grant me, I be- seech you, permission to travel to Madrid to fetch the Infanta, whom you have chosen for my consort, but who, I feel assured, never will be mine unless I can thus obtain her. Instead of quenching the passion I have conceived for this adorable princess, the difficulties which have occurred during the long-protracted negotiation for her hand, have in- creased it. I shall never be happy without her, and indeed have vowed to take no other wife, so that, unless I win her, I shall be condemned to a life of celibacy, and your royal line will not be continued."

"Saints forfend !" cried James, uneasily.

"In proceeding in person to fetch my bride," pursued Charles, "I shall imitate the example of my chivalrous ancestor, James V. of Scotland, who, journeying into France in quest of a consort, was rewarded by the hand of the Princess Madeleine, sole daughter of François I. Moreover, I shall copy, as I am bound to do, my wise and honoured father, whose ardent nature prompted him to sail to Denmark to gain the princess on whom he had set his affections. As James V. succeeded, and as you succeeded, sire, so shall I."

"Ahem !" exclaimed James, coughing dryly. "Dinna be guided by bonnie Jamie, Babie Charlie —dinna be guided by me. The wisest of men sometimes err, and I gave nae great proof of sagacity in taking that step."

"You gave unquestionable proof of spirit and of devotion to the queen my mother, sire," returned Charles. "Whatever the motive that influenced you, I honour you for it. But vouchsafe an answer to my request. Have I your permission to travel to Madrid?"

"Ye hae ta'en me so much by surprise that I can make nae direct response," returned James, cautiously. "The matter requires great consideration. When do you desire to set out?"

"Without delay—to-morrow," replied Charles.

"To-morrow!" ejaculated the king. "By my halidame! ye must be daft to think of it. Why, it will tak a month to fit out a fleet to convey ye to Spain! Ask Steenie, who is Lord High Admiral, and he will explain to you the time it will take to get all ready."

"I need not ask the question, sire, since it is not my intention to go to Spain in that princely fashion. I design to travel by post, in disguise, as a simple gentleman, accompanied only by Buckingham, who has consented to go with me, and two or three attendants."

"Wha the deil has put this mad scheme into your head?" cried James, aghast. "Ride by post frae London to Madrid, like a courier! Is it befitting the heir to the throne of England to travel sae? Answer me that, Babie Charlie? Answer me that?"

"I shall travel incognito, sire, and shall not discover myself till I reach Madrid."

"Ye'll never reach Madrid if ye travel in that way, my puir bairn," said the king. "Hae ye reflectit on the perils of the journey? Grantin' ye get safely through France, whilk I mich misdoubt, ye will hae to cross great barren plains and steep mountains infested by robbers, and may be set upon in some spot where there is nae chance of succour, and barbarously murthered, and then I shall lose my twa darling boys, Babie Charles and Steenie. Say nae mair aboot it—spare your breath —nae arguments will move me."

"I shall not arise till you grant my request, sire," returned Charles, maintaining his position. "I go like a paladin of old to win the sovereign mistress of my heart, and were the expedition unattended by danger, I would not undertake it."

"Why, ye are as moonstruck as Don Quixote himself!" cried James. "But dinna suppose yer auld dad will suffer ye to commit such folly. He loves his bairn too dearly. What say you, Steenie?" he added to Buckingham. "Surely ye canna be party to this hair-brained scheme?"

"If the prince travels to Madrid as he desires to do, I shall accompany him," returned Buckingham. "Your paternal anxiety magnifies the dangers of the journey. I warrant me you will laugh heartily at our adventures when we come back."

"If ye ever *do* come back, dear lads, I promise ye I shall laugh, and that right heartily," said James. "But something tells me if ye gang to Spain in this way, I shall never set eyes on ye mair. Why not tarry for the fleet? Besides, I darena consent without consulting the council, and they may prohibit my son's departure."

"Very likely they would, sire," observed Charles. "But you have pledged me your royal word not to mention the matter to any one without my consent; and I hold you strictly to the promise."

"Idiot that I was to bind myself sae!" cried the king. "But ye will gain naething by the stratagem—naething. I refuse my consent."

"Then the prince's death will lie at your door," rejoined Buckingham. "It will break his heart if he loses the Infanta—as he infallibly will, unless this expedient be adopted. Do I exaggerate, prince?—Speak!"

"Not in the least," replied Charles. "If I am thwarted, and robbed of my prize, I shall never survive the bitter disappointment."

"Was ever king sae sair beset?" groaned James. "I see plain eneuch that ye are baith in a plot against me, but ye shallna prevail. I am firm in my refusal."

" Hear me before you decide, sire," said Charles. " As Heaven shall judge me, if I am denied the Infanta, I will take no other wife. Your majesty professes to desire the marriage——"

" Professes to desire it!" interrupted James. " I desire naething on earth sae mich. I wad gie half my kingdom to accomplish it."

" Then let me go, and it is done," said Charles. " Hear me yet further, sire. Not only will my presence at Madrid bring the negotiation to an immediate and satisfactory issue, but it will ensure the restitution of his hereditary dominions to my brother-in-law, the Count Palatine. Philip IV. cannot refuse his aid to the Elector when I ask it."

" That wad, indeed, be a triumph gained, and wad gladden my heart, which is sair troubled in regard to my daughter Elizabeth," observed James. " I ought not to yield, for I hae mony misgivings as to the result of the expedition; but since ye are bent upon it, I will not hinder ye."

His point being thus gained, Charles sprang joyfully to his feet, and threw himself into his father's arms, who tenderly embraced him, exclaiming, " Heaven bless ye, my bonnie bairn, and grant ye a prosperous journey!"

" Your majesty's decision has been wisely made, and you will never rue it," observed Buckingham. " And now, since the affair is settled, it may be well to discuss the arrangements of the journey. We would defer to your majesty's opinion in the choice of our attendants. Whom do you recommend?"

" I need not search far to find one," returned James. " There is your secretary, Sir Francis Cottington, Babie Charlie, whom we have just elevated to a baronetcy. He has been attached to our embassy at Madrid, and knows the court intimately. You canna do better than take him. Sir Francis is a trusty and discreet man, in whom I have every confidence."

" Your confidence is well bestowed, sire," returned the prince. "I had fixed upon Cottington as one of my attendants, provided my project met with your sanction. He is without, in the ante-chamber; but he knows nothing of the enterprise, for neither Buckingham nor myself have breathed a word of it to any one save your majesty."

"I will talk to him anon," observed the king. "Then there is your groom of the chamber, Endymion Porter, who has just returned frae Madrid. He speaks the language like a Spaniard, kens the people weel, and will be verra useful to you. Take him."

"Willingly—right willingly," returned Charles. "I had also thought of Endymion Porter. His perfect knowledge of the language, and familiarity with the manners of the people, will be a great help to us. As your majesty is aware, I speak Spanish indifferently well myself."

"And I very indifferently," remarked Buckingham. "But I make no doubt we shall get on well enough. Your majesty having assigned Cottington and Endymion Porter to the prince, I will crave permission to take as my own attendant my master of the horse, Sir Richard Graham."

"I approve your choice, Steenie," replied James. "Dick Græme is as handsome as Adonis, and his bra' looks and gallant bearing will charm the Spanish señoras. Like Babie Charlie, he may chance to find a wife in Madrid. But hauld! there is one point which must not be forgotten. Does Dick speak Spanish?"

"Better than I do myself," returned Buckingham.

"That's na sayin' mich," laughed the king. "And now, lads, under what names do you mean to travel?"

"We have not thought of that," replied the prince. "Give us our designations, sire."

"The Palmerin de Inglaterra and Amadis de Gaula would suit ye best," said James, laughing; "but since these renowned names might prove inconvenient, I wad counsel you to adopt humbler appellations, and style yourselves the twa Smiths —Jock and Tam."

"Excellent!" cried Buckingham. "Your majesty has a rare humour. The prince shall be Jack Smith, and I will be Tom."

"I am quite content," remarked Charles. "As the Brothers Smith we will travel to Madrid."

"Will ye not send on a courier before you?" observed the king, pleased with their ready assent to his whim.

"That were to proclaim our secret to all the world," returned Charles. "None save our attendants must be made acquainted with our intended journey. There must be no avant courier to Paris or Madrid, or the project will be blown abroad and defeated. We must take Philip and Olivarez by surprise. On our arrival at Madrid, we will proceed at once to the English embassy."

"The hotel in which Bristol resides, and where you will find him, has an odd name," remarked James. "It is called *La Casa de las siete*

Chimeneas, or, in plain English, 'The House of Seven Chimneys.' Though so scantily supplied with chimneys, I believe it is a large mansion, sae ye will be weel accommodated; and I trust ye will gar every chimney reek while ye stay there."

"We will take good care of ourselves, never fear, sire," said Buckingham. "I like the name of the house. Seven is a lucky number. There are the Seven Sages of Greece—the Seven Champions—the Seven Stars—why not the Seven Chimneys?"

"One of the Pleiades has vanished," remarked James. "Count the chimneys when ye get to Madrid, and let me know that all are standing, for if ane be wanting, I shall think that your errand will prove unsuccessful. Ye said just now that Sir Francis Cottington is in the ante-chamber. Bid him come in. As he is to attend you, I may talk the matter over with him, I suppose?"

"Most assuredly, sire," replied Charles. "I should wish you to do so."

"Call him in, Steenie—call him in," said the king; "and if Endymion Porter and Dick Græme chance to be in the ante-chamber, let them come in at the same time."

"All three were there when his highness and myself passed through," returned Buckingham. "Cottington will oppose the expedition," he added, in a whisper, to Charles.

"He will not dare to do so when he finds I am bent upon it," rejoined the prince, in the same tone.

"We shall see," observed Buckingham, as he stepped towards the door to execute the king's order.

II.

SHOWING WHO WERE CHOSEN AS JACK AND TOM SMITH'S
ATTENDANTS ON THE JOURNEY.

FINDING that the three persons he sought were still in the ante-chamber, Buckingham directed the gentleman-usher in attendance to summon them, and, this being done, in another minute they were brought into the presence.

Sir Francis Cottington, who was first to enter, was of middle age, being born in 1576. Of a good Somersetshire family, after serving as secretary to Sir Philip Strafford during the reign of Elizabeth, he became attached to the embassy to

Spain, and his long residence at Madrid had given him the look of a Spaniard, which was heightened by his olive complexion, dark eyes, and jet-black moustache and beard. His habiliments were of murrey-coloured velvet, and a long Toledo hung from his side. As previously intimated, Sir Francis Cottington was now secretary to Prince Charles, and was, moreover, much in the king's confidence, who constantly consulted him about Spanish affairs, and was generally guided by his advice.

Endymion Porter came next. He was somewhat younger than Cottington, but though not so polished in manner or intelligent-looking as the prince's secretary, he had a pleasant countenance, and a goodly person.

The last to pay reverence to the king was an exceedingly handsome young man. Selected on account of his good looks and agreeable manner to the post of master of the horse, which he filled in Buckingham's princely household, Sir Richard

Graham, by the elegance of his attire and personal graces, excited almost as much admiration as his magnificent patron. He was as tall as Buckingham, who was upwards of six feet high, but more powerfully built than the marquis. Graham's features were regular, and of classical mould, his complexion bright and fresh, his eyes dark blue, his locks brown and curled liked those of Antinous, his beard and moustaches of the same hue, and his teeth superb. Sir Richard was a few months younger than Prince Charles, and had recently been knighted by the king at Buckingham's instance.

Glancing round at the trio, James said, "I hae sent for ye, sirs, on a maist important matter, but, before confiding it to ye, I charge ye on your allegiance that ye keep it a profound secret. Mark weel what I say—a profound secret."

"Your majesty may rely upon us," returned the persons addressed.

"Weel, then," continued the king, "I will tell

ye what it is without mair ado. Babie Charles and Steenie hae resolved to travel post to Madrid, to fetch the Infanta. Never stare, sirs—never stare! as if ye thought I were jesting—it's the truth. They mean to travel post, I tell ye, incognito, and with only three attendants, and have made choice of you."

This unexpected intelligence produced a marked effect on the hearers. All three were surprised by it, and Cottington trembled so violently, that he could scarcely support himself.

"What ails ye, Sir Francis?" cried James. "Dinna ye like the expedition?"

"Of a truth, my liege, I do not," replied Cottington; "and I would fain dissuade his highness from so hazardous an undertaking. I know the Spaniards well, and am therefore sensible of the risk he will incur."

"Ye hear that, Babie Charles?" cried James. "Sir Francis is an honest man, and speaks truth, however distasteful it may be, without fear. He is of our ain opinion."

"I have already told your majesty that I am determined to go, be the danger what it may," said Charles, glancing sternly at his secretary as he spoke. "I should be loth to take Sir Francis with me against his will."

"Let him stay behind," cried Buckingham. "How say you, sirs?" he added to the two others. "Are you content to go with us?"

"I shall be proud and happy to attend his highness and your grace," rejoined Endymion Porter; "and I see no risk whatever in the expedition. The prince will be heartily welcomed by his Spanish majesty—of that I am well assured."

"For my part, I shall account it a great distinction to share, however humbly, in an enterprise so heroic," observed Sir Richard Graham. "The proposed expedition is, in all respects, suited to a prince so chivalrous as his highness, and I marvel not that he desires to undertake it. Danger enhances the glory of any great achievement, and, should peril occur, we shall know how to encounter it."

"Well spoken, Dick," cried Buckingham. "It is only Cottington who fears danger."

"It is my devotion to the prince that fills me with apprehension, and prompts me to dissuade him from the journey," returned Cottington. "If his highness will not heed my warning, I am ready to go with him, to guide him, and strive to protect him from peril, but I cannot reconcile it to myself to hold my tongue when advice may be useful."

"No more of this, sir," cried Charles, angrily.

"Nay, chide him not, Babie Charlie, he means weel," interposed James. "What hae ye to say, Sir Francis? Speak out, man—speak out—I command ye!"

"Since your majesty lays your injunctions upon

me, I must obey," replied Cottington. "Not only do I feel that the expedition will be attended with many risks, but so far from promoting the match, I am confident it will put an end to it. Should the prince be so rash as to place himself in the hands of the Spaniards, they will make fresh demands, and detain him till their exactions are complied with. Assured of this, I deem it incumbent upon me to warn his highness before he runs headlong into the trap. The grand aim of the Spanish cabinet is to advance the Romish faith in England, and this they will be enabled to do, if the prince delivers himself into their hands."

"Ye are right, Sir Francis—ye are right," cried James. "I see it a' now. The step would be fatal, but, Heaven be praised, it is not yet ta'en! If the Spaniards ance get possession of ye, Babie Charlie, the Pope will be able to dictate his ain terms, and will make the restitution of his spee-ritual power and the restoration of the Romish faith the price of your release."

"This is idle, sire," remarked Charles. "I have too much faith in Spanish honour to doubt for a moment the treatment I shall experience from Philip IV. Spain is the most chivalrous country in Europe."

"But the most perfidious," cried the king. "I will not trust my bairn to traitors. I willna let you go."

"If you violate your promise, sire, you must take the consequences," rejoined Charles, sternly. "I swear to you I will never marry."

"But, my ain bairn——"

"I swear it," repeated Charles, emphatically.

"If your majesty breaks a promise thus solemnly made," said Buckingham, contemptuously, "no credit will in future be attached to aught you may assert. Your word is passed, and cannot be recalled."

"Hear me, Steenie—hear me, Babie Charlie! I implore you baith to listen to me!" cried the king.

"Nothing you can say will move me, sire," rejoined Buckingham, haughtily. "Such vacillation is unworthy of you. As to you, Cottington," he added, in a menacing tone, "you will repent your mischievous interference."

"Even if I should be unlucky enough to forfeit his highness's favour as well as yours, my lord, I shall never repent what I have done," replied Cottington. "As a faithful servant of the prince, I am bound to endeavour to deter him from a step which I feel may be fraught with fatal consequences. Having discharged my duty, I have nothing more to say. It is for his majesty to decide."

"Release me frae my promise, Babie Charlie! —release me, Steenie!" cried James, in almost piteous accents.

But both looked at him coldly and contemptuously, and neither made reply.

At this moment a head, covered with a fool's cap, surmounted by a coxcomb, was thrust from out the tapestry opposite the king, and a mocking voice exclaimed, " Ye seem perplexed, gossip. Will ye take a fool's advice?"

" What, hast thou been playing the spy upon us, Archie?" exclaimed the king, by no means displeased at the interruption. "Come forth instanter, sirrah!"

Thus exhorted, a fantastic little personage, clad in motley, holding a bauble, and having a droll, though somewhat malicious expression of countenance, stepped forth from his place of concealment. It was the court jester, Archie Armstrong.

" Hast thou been there all the time, knave?" demanded James.

"Ay, gossip," returned Archie, "and I have not lost a word of the discourse. I approve of Babie Charlie's visit to Spain, but he must take my cap with him, and if Philip allows him to come back, he may leave it as a parting gift to his majesty."

"Tell me what I shall do, Archie?" cried the king. "I am well-nigh at my wits' end."

"Then are you close to folly, gossip," returned Archie. "But since you ask me, I will tell you what you must *not* do. Break not your word, or you will never more be trusted."

"Right, fool," said Buckingham, approvingly.

"Balk not the prince your son's humour," pursued Archie, "or you will never have a daughter-in-law."

"Excellent counsel," said Charles. "Wisdom proceeds from the lips of fools."

"Make up your mind to what cannot be helped, gossip," said Archie to the king. "Babie Charlie and Steenie *will* go to Madrid, and there is no use in saying them nay; you had best yield with a good grace."

James seemed to be of this opinion, for, after a brief pause, he exclaimed:

"Aweel, my bairns, I can hauld out nae longer.

E'en gang your gait; and may gude come of the journey."

"Folly, you see, has carried the day," said Archie to Cottington.

Having thus regained their ground, the prince and Buckingham overwhelmed the old monarch with thanks, terming him the most indulgent of fathers and the best of kings. These demonstrations brought tears to James's eyes — tears of dotage, Buckingham thought them.

"Buss me, Babie Charlie, buss me," cried James, tenderly embracing his son. "Ah! ye little heed, my bonnie bairn, what pangs ye are about to inflict on your auld dad. But why not delay your departure for a few days? I hae mich to think of—my mind is sair distraught the noo— mich advice to gie you."

"There is far more danger in delay than in the journey itself," observed Charles, well knowing that a few hours might cause a change in his father's disposition. "We shall start at an early hour to-morrow morning. Meantime, with your gracious permission, we will send Cottington and Endymion Porter to Dover, to hire a vessel to transport us to Boulogne."

"Weel, weel, it shall be sae," groaned James —"but what a tempting of Providence to trust the hope of the kingdom to a frail shallop! If ill betide, I shall have meikle to answer for."

"Cottington will provide us with a stout ship, and the wind will favour us, sire," said Charles, "so you need be under no apprehension for our safety."

"I see 'tis in vain to reason wi' ye," returned his father. "Gang to Dover as fast as ye can, Sir Francis," he added to Cottington, "and tak Endymion Porter wi' ye. Hire a good ship for the voyage."

"Set out with all despatch, I pray you, Cottington," said Charles. "You will obtain funds for the journey from my comptroller. Have all ready for our embarkation on Wednesday morning. We trust to be at Dover to-morrow night."

"All shall be ready for your highness," replied Cottington. "I now take leave of your majesty."

"Fare ye weel, my faithful Cottington," said James, giving him his hand to kiss. "Ye will hae a precious charge. I needna bid ye tak care of my bairns."

Cottington said nothing, but bowing profoundly to his majesty, quitted the cabinet with Endymion Porter.

Scarcely was he gone than James cried out hastily, "Stop them!—stop them! I hae something more to say."

"Impossible, sire," rejoined Buckingham, who justly dreaded lest the king should veer back to the old quarter. "If you have any further directions to give, we will attend to them. But let me pray your majesty to regard our project more cheerfully. You will have us back with the Infanta before Whitsuntide, and then I warrant me you will commend us for the exploit."

"Ye are more sanguine than I am, Steenie,"

groaned the king. "I never look to see either of ye again, and that makes me sae sad."

"Think of the bonnie princess, with her rich dowry, gossip," said Archie. "I guess you will be glad to see her. Think of your son-in-law, the Count Palatine, and how rejoiced he will be at the restitution of his dominions."

"I believe thou art in the plot against me, sirrah," said the king, cheering up a little. "And now, my bairns," he continued, "though ye winna let me send aught *afore* ye to Madrid, or procure ye a safe-conduct through France frae our ambassador, Sir Edward Herbert, I shall not fail to send *after* ye a' ye may need to grace ye at the court of Madrid, as braw apparel, jewels, horses, and the like. I dinna doubt but half my court will follow ye."

"Prithee, gossip, let me go with the prince's train," entreated Archie.

"Nay, I shall need thee to divert my melancholy," returned James.

"I shall add to your dulness, an you detain me, gossip," rejoined Archie. "All my mirth will vanish."

"Then have thy will, and gae," rejoined James. Then turning to his son and Buckingham, he added, "Be not afeared that ony tidings of your departure will reach France for some days, for on Wednesday I will stop all couriers, and lay an embargo on all vessels bound to ony French port. And now once more adieu, my bonnie bairns. Sair I am to lose you, but greeting will not mend the matter." So saying, he tenderly embraced them both, and bestowed his blessing upon them.

On quitting his father, Charles manifested considerable emotion, but Buckingham took leave of his royal master with apparent unconcern.

As Sir Richard Graham made a reverence to the king before following them, James said to him, "I hae a question to ask ye, Dick, and I require a straightforward answer. Are ye wholly unfettered, man—eh?"

"I do not exactly understand your majesty," returned the young man.

"Then ye are duller than I thought. Hae ye breathed vows to ony fair dame or damsel at our court? Hae ye tied love-knots? Ye are of an amorous complexion, and like eneuch to hae a sweetheart. Hae ye ony engagement?"

"No, sire," replied Graham. "In that respect I am as free as air."

"Then tak my advice, man, and bring back a rich Spanish wife wi' ye," said James.

"I will endeavour to obey your majesty," replied Graham.

And with a fresh reverence he followed the prince and Buckingham out of the cabinet, leaving the king alone with Archie.

III.

HOW TOM AND JACK SET OUT ON THEIR JOURNEY; AND HOW THEY GOT TO THE FERRY NEAR TILBURY FORT.

LATER in the day, in pursuance of the plan arranged between him and the prince, Buckingham quitted York House, and, attended by Sir Richard Graham, repaired to New Hall, in Essex—a noble mansion, which he had purchased only two years previously from the Earl of Sussex, to whose brother it had been granted by Queen Elizabeth.

Situated between Chelmsford and Waltham Abbey, and surrounded by an extensive park, well stocked with deer, and boasting much fine timber, New-Hall had been a favourite hunting-seat of Henry VIII., who termed it, from the beauty of the site, Beaulieu. It was a vast structure, consisting of two large quadrangles, and possessed, among other stately chambers, a grand banqueting-hall, nearly a hundred feet in length, and proportionately wide and lofty, in which bluff King Hal had often feasted on the venison killed in the park, and which was still adorned with his arms sculptured in stone. James I. delighted in New-Hall, and counselled his favourite to buy the mansion, probably providing the funds for the purchase, and here he often visited Buckingham, chasing the deer in the park, and carousing in the great hall.

While Buckingham proceeded to his country-seat, Charles started for Theobalds, where he remained till evening, when he rode with but slight attendance to New-Hall. On arriving at his destination he sent back his attendants, telling them he should remain in privacy with his lordship of

Buckingham for two or three days, and giving one of them a letter to be conveyed next morning to the king. The singularity of this step excited some surprise among the prince's attendants, and they hazarded many guesses at the motive of this sudden visit to New-Hall. All these conjectures, however, were wide of the truth. Charles was very unceremoniously welcomed by Buckingham. They supped together in the great hall, but without state, and were only attended by Sir Richard Graham—the serving-men standing out of earshot —and almost immediately after the meal, the marquis and his royal guest retired to rest. All needful preparations for the journey were entrusted to Graham, who delightedly undertook the task.

Long before daylight next morning, the two adventurous companions were called by Graham, who assisted the prince to attire himself in a riding-dress of far plainer stuff than he had ever worn before, and this office performed, the young knight went to render the same service to his patron, but found it needless, Buckingham being already fully equipped in a suit exactly resembling that of the prince.

A few minutes later, when Charles and his favourite met in a chamber where a collation had been laid overnight, they surveyed each other for a moment in silence, and then burst into laughter at the change wrought in their appearance, as well by their apparel as by the false beards with which they had disguised their features. Sir Richard Graham, who was standing by, shared in their merriment. He was similarly habited, and his riding-dress, which was of dark green cloth, with boots drawn up above the knee, became him extremely well, but he had not deemed it necessary to mask his handsome countenance as the others had done.

"Will it please your highness to taste this capon?" he said, as Charles sat down at table.

"Help me—but give me no title, Dick," replied the prince. "Till I reach Madrid, I have laid aside my rank, and am now plain Jack Smith."

"And I am his brother Tom—forget not that, Dick," added Buckingham.

"Furthermore, thou art licensed to sit in our presence," pursued Charles. "During the journey we are equals."

Notwithstanding this gracious permission, Sir Richard hesitated to avail himself of it, but Buckingham enforcing the order, he took a seat, and all ceremony being now laid aside, he proceeded to lay in a good stock of the viands spread out before him.

"I would I had as good an appetite as thou hast, Dick," cried the prince, admiring his prowess. "I have vainly tried to get through this capon's wing, while thou hast made tremendous havoc with the pasty."

"I have not half done yet, your highness—I mean Master Jack Smith, pardon the involuntary slip of the tongue—the fact is, I have slept little, and find myself frightfully hungry."

"Then satisfy thyself, but use despatch, for we must away presently," remarked Buckingham. "Thou may'st eat both for my brother Jack and myself, for I have as sorry an appetite as he. Take a cup of sack, Jack, to the success of our expedition."

"With all my heart," replied Charles, filling a goblet, while Graham followed their example. "The wine has done me good," pursued the prince. "Hast thou finished, thou insatiable glutton?"

"Another moment," responded Graham, hastily disposing of a slice of ham, and swallowing another cup of sack. "There, now I am quite ready. I will go fetch the valises, which are all carefully packed."

So saying he disappeared, but almost instantly returned with the baggage, while the prince and Buckingham, being already booted and spurred, took up their broad-leaved hats, cloaks, and horse-whips, and, moving as noiselessly as they could, proceeded to a private staircase which conducted them to a postern-door. This door being unlocked by Buckingham, the party found themselves in the garden, but marching quickly, under the guidance of Graham, they threaded a long yew-tree alley, .and soon reached an outlet into the park. On issuing forth, notwithstanding the obscurity, for it was not yet light, they could distinguish three mounted grooms, each of whom held a horse by the bridle.

Without a word, Charles vaulted into the saddle of the steed nearest him, Buckingham followed his example, while Graham, consigning the valises to the groom, was instantly on the back of the third horse.

Just as they started, a clock placed in an inner court of the hall struck five.

In another moment the trio, attended by the grooms, were galloping down a sweeping glade, skirted by lordly trees, then of course bereft of half their beauty, from want of foliage.

While they were thus speeding along, Buckingham remarked that the prince's looks were fixed on the heavens, and he asked what he was gazing at?

"At yon star," replied Charles. "'Tis hers!"

"It heralds you on to Madrid," said the marquis.

"Perchance it is shining upon her at this moment," cried Charles, with all a lover's rapture.

"Like enough, if her casement be open," rejoined Buckingham.

Charles did not hear the remark, but exclaimed, aloud:

"Mistress of my heart! life of my life! I am about to seek thee in a foreign land, and will not return till I can bring thee back with me."

Blissful visions rose before him, and he fell into a reverie, which lasted till they were out of the park.

A narrow lane brought them to the high road

to Chelmsford. Pursuing this till they got within a short distance of the town, they struck into a by-road on the left, and, fording the Chelmer at Moulsham, shaped their course through a series of lanes, passing by Badow, Sandon, and Hanning-field, until at last they mounted the hill on which Bellericay is perched.

Though still wanting an hour to sunrise, it had become sufficiently light to enable them, from the eminence they had gained, plainly to discern the broad river they designed to cross, and the Kentish hills on the opposite bank. Turning their gaze in this direction, they fancied they could even distinguish Gravesend. Before entering Bellericay they dismounted, and, consigning their horses to the grooms, dismissed the men, with strict injunctions of silence.

"An ye breathe a word of what has occurred, your tongues shall be cut out," said Buckingham; "but if ye are discreet, ye shall be well rewarded."

As the grooms rode off, Charles and Buckingham proceeded towards the Crown Inn, where post-horses were to be had, followed by Graham, carrying the baggage.

At the door of the hostel stood a waggon with a long team of horses, and several persons were collected around to witness the departure of the vehicle for London.

Seeing this, the prince and Buckingham halted, leaving Graham to go on and order the horses. As the young man approached the house, he was addressed by a sharp-looking little personage, who proved to be Master Ephraim Cogswell, the host.

"Good morrow, fair sir," said Cogswell, doffing his cap. "Are you going by the waggon? If so, you are just in time."

"No, friend," replied Graham. "Myself and my masters are not bound for London, but for Rochester, and we want post-horses to take us to Tilbury Fort, whence we propose to cross the

Thames to Gravesend. We shall need a postboy
to attend us, and carry the baggage."

"How many are ye, master? Ha! I see," he
added, noticing Charles and Buckingham in the
distance. And, after giving the necessary orders
to an ostler, bidding him use despatch, he added,
"May I make so bold as to ask how your masters
are named, sir? They cannot be of this neighbourhood, for I remember them not, though I
think I have seen your face before."

"Like enough," returned Graham. "It is not
the first time I have been at Bellericay. My
masters are the two Smiths."

At this moment the landlord was called by a
passenger in the waggon, and shortly afterwards
the vehicle was set in motion, and proceeded on
its way. The host then returned to the charge.

"You said that your masters are named Smith,
sir," he remarked to Graham. "Are they of this
county?"

"You are inquisitive, mine host," returned

Graham. "They are the brothers Smith, of Saffron Walden, and are tanners by trade. I am their man."

"They don't look much like tanners, friend," observed Cogswell, "nor you like a tanner's man. However, it's no business of mine. But here come the hackneys."

And, as he spoke, the horses were brought out of the stable, ready saddled and bridled. Seeing which, Charles and Buckingham came forward.

"No more tanners than I am a tanner," murmured Cogswell, eyeing them narrowly as they approached. "I will consent to have my own hide curried if they be not noblemen. Give your lordships good day," he added, bowing respectfully to them.

"Lordships! What means the fellow?" cried Buckingham. "Hast thou been jesting with him, Dick?" he added to Graham.

"Ay, that he has," returned Cogswell. "He avouched that your lordships bore the common name of Smith, and were nothing better than tanners. But that won't pass with me. Ephraim Cogswell can tell a nobleman when he sees him. And, but for your lordship's black beard, I would venture to affirm that I am standing in the presence of the Marquis of Buckingham himself."

"You are mistaken, friend," returned the marquis, "and I counsel you not to repeat that pleasantry, as if it chance to reach the ears of my lord of Buckingham, he is likely to resent the liberty taken with his name."

"Nay, I meant no offence," replied Cogswell, bowing. "I know how to hold my tongue."

Somewhat annoyed by this occurrence, Charles and Buckingham mounted their horses and rode off, and were followed by Graham and a postboy, with the baggage.

Passing through the town, the party kept on the ridge of the hill for some distance, and then descended to Little Bursted. In less than an hour from quitting Bellericay, after crossing Langdon

Hill, and passing over Horndon Hill, they reached Tilbury Fort, where quitting their horses, and paying the postboy, they instantly embarked on board the ferry-boat, and ordered the two men in charge of it to convey them with all despatch to Gravesend.

IV.

HOW JACK AND TOM WERE TAKEN FOR HIGHWAYMEN ON GAD'S HILL.

THE morning was clear but cold, and a strong north-easterly wind ruffled the water, and sent the ferry-boat quickly along. The passage across the river was not without interest to Jack and Tom. Wrapping their cloaks around them to screen them from the blast, they amused themselves, in the first instance, by examining Tilbury Fort, which seemed to menace them with its guns. They next gazed admiringly down the wide and long reach called " the Hope," skirted on one side by the white cliffs of Kent, and on the other by the woody hills of Essex; then noted the appearance and manœuvres of some passing vessels; and lastly, as they neared Gravesend, turned their attention to the blockhouse, battery, and wharf, and commented upon the ships, some of considerable burden, lying off the port.

While his leaders were thus occupied, Graham, in order to pass the time, entered into conversation with the master ferryman, a weather-beaten old fellow named Randal Fowler, and praised the quickness of his boat.

"Ay, ay, she is a gallant little craft, sure enough," replied the ferryman. "She has done wonders in her day, and, moreover, has had some great folks aboard of her."

"Indeed, what great personages have you had the luck to carry?"

"Marry, the greatest was the Lord High Admiral," returned Randal.

"Nonsense, man, you don't mean to say that the

Lord High Admiral has used your boat?" cried Graham, glancing at Buckingham.

"Yes I do, master," replied the ferryman, proudly.

"I don't recollect the circumstance, fellow," remarked Buckingham; "that is," he added, correcting himself, "I never heard that the Lord High Admiral had crossed the river by this ferry."

"It wasn't here, but in the Medway, that his lordship used my boat," rejoined Randal. "I took him and the Earl of Rutland to see the ships lying at Sheerness. I shan't forget it, for I got a piece of gold for the job. May I make so bold as to ask whither you are bound, masters?"

"For France," replied Buckingham, in a tone calculated to put an end to further inquiries.

But old Randal was not to be checked, and he was about to ask further questions, when Graham observed to him, in a low tone:

" Don't trouble the gentlemen further. They are going across the water to fight a duel."

" Can't they cut each other's throats, if they are so minded, in this country?" observed Randal. " It seems a waste of time and money to go so far on such an errand. However, that's no concern of mine."

With this he proceeded to let down the sail, calling to his man to look out, and in a few minutes more they were close to the landing-place. When Graham took out his purse to pay the fare, he could find no silver within it, and his companions were unable to assist him. They had all plenty of gold, but no small change. Old Randal had only a few pence in his greasy leather pouch, and as to changing a jacobus, that was out of the question.

" Give him a couple of gold pieces," cried Buckingham. " We can't be detained a moment in landing."

As Graham obeyed the order, and placed the

glittering coin in Randal's horny hands, the old ferryman exclaimed, in tones that bespoke his gratitude, "I heartily thank your honours. You are generous as princes—far more generous than the Lord High Admiral. This is the best fare I ever got, and if I could only earn as much every time I cross the Thames, I should soon be rich. Take an old man's advice, and make up your quarrel. You are goodly gentlemen both, and it would be a thousand pities if either of you were harmed."

"Hold thy peace, friend," said Graham, stopping him. "Thou hast got more than thy deserts. Be content."

"I am content—more than content," persisted Randal; "but I would fain prevent bloodshed. Beseech ye, good sirs, to listen to me."

But he spoke to deaf ears, for no sooner did the boat touch the strand than the prince and Buckingham leaped ashore, and ran up the steps, passing as quickly as they could through the crowd of seafaring men and others collected on the wharf. They were speedily followed by Graham, charged with the baggage, for he resolutely refused the offer of Randal to carry it for him, not wishing to be troubled further with the old man. The party at once proceeded to the Falcon, where post-horses were kept.

As soon as his passengers were gone, old Randal took out the two jacobuses he had received, and, while feasting his eyes upon them, he thought it would be a lasting reproach to him if he allowed the duel to take place; and coming to the conclusion that the kindest and most Christian thing he could do was to have the gentlemen arrested, and bound over to keep the peace towards each other, he left his boat, and went to inform the portreve, as the chief officer of the town was designated, of the matter that had come to his knowledge.

The portreve, fully believing his story, at once despatched two officers to the Falcon to arrest the intending combatants, and bring them before him; but, on arriving at the post-house, the officers found that the persons of whom they were in quest had started full a quarter of an hour before. However, as the portreve's orders were peremptory, they ordered post-horses, and set off after the travellers, and being well mounted, made sure of overtaking them before they could reach Rochester.

Meanwhile, the three companions, attended as before by a postboy carrying their baggage, had passed through the rich gardens surrounding the town, mounted the windmill-crowned heights, whence such an extensive and beautiful prospect is obtained, had ridden on through Chalk-street and past the thick woods of Maplesden, and did not slacken their pace till they reached the foot of Gad's Hill.

"Here we are at Gad's Hill—the scene of one of Falstaff's exploits," quoth Tom to Jack, as they were slowly ascending the eminence. "Hereabouts, the fat knight, with Bardolph and Peto, robbed the travellers of the gold they were conveying to the king's exchequer, and here the rogues, in their turn, were stripped of their booty and soundly belaboured by the madcap Prince Hal, and Poins. But even in our own day," added Tom, " Gad's Hill has an ill repute, and these thickets are still haunted by knights of the post and minions of the moon, who sally forth to bid the traveller stand and deliver, on peril of his life. Heaven grant we meet with no such caitiffs! Were they to ease us of the twenty-five thousand pounds we carry with us in bills of exchange on Paris and Madrid, besides our gold, they would obtain a rich spoil, and might hinder our journey."

" Prithee, not so loud, Tom," said Jack, glancing around suspiciously—" you may be overheard; and though I delight in adventures, I have no fancy for an encounter with highwaymen."

" Let us push on, then, Jack," rejoined Tom. " As I have just told you, this is a dangerous spot."

Putting their horses in motion, they soon reached the brow of the hill. Here, on the left of the road, stood a small hostel, called the Leather Bottle, and as Jack, who was charmed with the beauty of the scene, halted for a moment, the postboy found time to drain a horn of humming ale. Presently the travellers resumed their journey, and were descending the hill, which on this side, as on the other, was covered by wood, when they descried a large coach drawn by four horses coming towards them. Near this carriage, and apparently conversing with some one inside it, rode a richly-attired gentleman, attended by three or four mounted lacqueys.

"By Heaven! Jack, that is one of the royal carriages!" exclaimed Tom, calling on the other to halt. "And do you not perceive that the person who is riding beside it is no other than Sir Lewis Lewkner? Plague take him! What can he be doing here? This is the last place where one

would expect to meet the master of the ceremonies."

"'Tis an unlucky chance that has brought him
here," cried Jack. "He is certain to recognise us.
We must turn back."

"No; let us put a bold front upon it, and dash
rapidly past the coach. We shall escape notice,"
cried Tom.

"Impossible!" returned Jack. "It is the Comte
de Tillières who is in the carriage. I caught a
glimpse of his features just this moment."

"You are right," observed Tom. "It is the
French ambassador. I saw him myself quite
plainly. Look! he is now thrusting his head
through the window."

"And see! they have stopped the carriage,
and are consulting together," cried Jack. "They
evidently take us for highwaymen, and are pre-
paring to resist our attack."

"Shall we attack them, Jack?" said Tom, gaily.

"To rob the French ambassador and the master of the ceremonies would be an exploit worthy of Prince Hal himself, and would be 'argument for a week, laughter for a month, and a good jest for ever.'"

"The matter is too serious for jesting," replied Jack, gravely. "Here comes Sir Lewis Lewkner. Shall we confront him, or beat a retreat?"

As he spoke, the master of the ceremonies rode towards them, with the evident intention of demanding their business. But they did not wait for his approach. Finding it impossible to avoid the encounter, which must have resulted in a discovery, Jack struck spurs into his horse, and leaping a low hedge on the right, plunged into the wood. Tom dashed after him, and Graham ordered the postboy to follow, but as the lad hesitated, he seized his horse, and, by a vigorous application of the whip, forced the animal to clear the hedge.

Just as this was accomplished, Sir Lewis Lewkner came up with the lacqueys, and called out, "Stand! if you are an honest man, and give an account of yourself!" Then, looking at the other more narrowly, he added, "Either my eyes deceive me, or it is Sir Richard Graham? But why this garb? Whom have you with you, Sir Richard?"

"Those are my friends, Jack and Tom Smith," roared Graham. And without another word, he jumped the hedge and disappeared in the thicket, leaving the master of the ceremonies completely bewildered. On recovering from his surprise, Sir Lewis returned to the coach, and told the ambassador what had occurred.

"A strange notion has come into my head," he added. "I feel confident that it was Sir Richard Graham whom I beheld, and I am almost equally certain that the persons with him, whom he called Jack and Tom Smith, were no other than the Prince of Wales and the Marquis of Buckingham."

"You amaze me," cried the Comte de Tillières. "The prince and Buckingham! in disguise, travelling under feigned names, and without attendants! This is the road to Dover. Parbleu! can they be going to France?"

"That is highly improbable, your excellency," returned Sir Lewis, who began to feel that he had said too much.

Nothing more passed till they reached the summit of the hill, when they perceived two men galloping towards them. These were the officers, who halted as they came up, and one of them, respectfully saluting Sir Lewis, inquired whether three gentlemen had passed them on the road; adding, that he had an order from the portreve of Gravesend for their arrest, as they were about to cross over to France to fight a duel.

" Aha! this proves they could not be the persons I suspected," observed Sir Lewis to the ambassador, who did not, however, appear entirely satisfied. " The gentlemen you are in pursuit of," added Lewkner to the officer, "avoided us, and took refuge in yonder wood. Possibly, they may have returned to the high road."

"Not a doubt of it," replied the officer.

"I should like to know the result of this adventure," observed the Comte de Tillières. "Go with these officers, Martin," he added to one of his mounted attendants, "and bring me word what happens. Thou wilt find me at Gravesend."

Adding a few words in a lower tone, he placed a purse in Martin's hands, and dismissed him.

As Martin galloped off with the officers, the coach was again put in motion, and the ambassador and Lewkner pursued their way towards Gravesend.

V.

HOW JACK AND TOM WERE PURSUED BY THE OFFICERS FROM GRAVESEND.

As had been conjectured, the travellers left the covert in which they had sought shelter and returned to the high road, speeding along it till they came to Strood Hill, from the summit of which they obtained a charming view of Rochester, with its ancient castle, its cathedral, and other picturesque structures, as well as of the adjacent town of Chatham, and the district watered by the winding Medway.

While they were pausing to examine this noble

prospect, the postboy warned them that they were pursued, and pointed out the two officers and Martin, who were scouring along the valley about a mile off. At this sight the travellers immediately started again, and, dashing down the hill, speedily reached Strood. Next crossing the old wooden bridge at Rochester, and entering that fair city —then, as now, one of the most picturesque and beautiful in England—they rode along the High-street, till they reached Chatham.

Their horses were in such good condition, that it was evident they could hold out for another stage, so, quitting Chatham, they mounted another lovely hill, from the summit of which a delightful and extensive view greeted them, comprehending almost the whole of the meandering Medway, with Standgate Creek, Sheerness, the Nore, and the distant coast of Essex.

Nearer at hand the prospect was yet more en-chanting, being composed of hill and dale, vil-lages, churches, and homesteads, hop-grounds, apple-orchards, cherry-orchards, and all that can contribute to the embellishment of an English landscape. Of course, at this season of the year, when the hop-grounds lacked their garniture, when the orchards had no ripe produce, when the fields were bare of crops, and the woods leafless, the picture was deprived of much of its charm. Still, even with these disadvantages, it was *so* beautiful, that Charles, as he gazed at it with a raptured eye, exclaimed:

"Drayton speaks truth when he says, in his 'Polyolbion,'

O famous Kent!
What county hath this Isle that may compare with thee!

Fairer scene than this cannot be imagined. Yon broad and winding river, hastening on to mingle its waters with those of the Thames before they both are lost in the sea—those charming hills—those pompous woods—those ancient mansions—those reverend fabrics—those towns and hamlets—

all bespeaking peace and plenteousness. Can any picture be more lovely?"

"None, none," replied Buckingham, who either felt or feigned a like enthusiasm. "It is only in England—perhaps only in this county—that such a prospect can be seen. We shall find nothing like it in Spain, you may depend, Jack. You must bring the Infanta to behold it."

"I shall not fail," replied Charles.

At this moment, Graham, who had been lingering behind, called out:

"Those rascally officers are coming quickly after us. They have not stopped at Rochester, as we expected, but have passed through Chatham, and are even now scaling this hill."

"Plague take the knaves!" cried Tom, impatiently. "Why should we concern ourselves about them?"

"They will cause us delay, and every hour—every minute—is of importance," returned Jack.

"Let us on. We shall reach Sittingbourne before them, and it is not likely they will proceed beyond that place."

" On, then, to Sittingbourne," cried Tom.

And the whole party rapidly descended the hill.

At the foot of the eminence, on a common, where a road branched off to Maidstone, stood a large triangular gibbet, from which dangled the grisly skeletons of three robbers who once haunted the neighbouring thickets, and had been the terror of all travellers on that way. With a glance of disgust at these loathly objects, Jack and his companions rode on through Hambley woods, past Rainham, through the old town of Newington, on the farther side of which they mounted Keycall Hill, descending upon Key-street, after which they came in sight of Milton, an ancient town famous for its oysters, and once possessing a palace built by Alfred, but subsequently destroyed by Earl Godwin in the reign of Edward the Confessor.

Farther on, they passed the remains of Castle

Rough, another fortress built by Alfred, and then entering Sittingbourne, rode at once to the Red Lion, and called for post-horses.

These were brought out with so much expedition, that the travellers were mounted and off full five minutes before their pursuers came up. Great disappointment was expressed by the latter on their arrival, and the officers would have relinquished the chase, but they were induced to go on by Martin, who paid for their post-horses, and promised to reward them liberally.

Jack and Tom were now three or four miles ahead, and had already passed Hempstead and Radfield, had cleared the little village of Green street, and were making their way, at a rapid pace, along Watling-street (the ancient Roman road), by Norton Ash, Stone, and Raven Hill, towards Ospringe.

While mounting Ospringe Hill, on which a beacon then stood, they cast a look towards Feversham, Davington, and the marshy tract adjoining the Swale, bringing the Bay of Whitstable within their ken.

From Ospringe, about twenty minutes' hard riding brought them to Boughton Hill, from the summit of which they obtained a magnificent view over the woody district known as the Forest of Blean. From this point they first descried the lofty tower of Canterbury Cathedral rising above the woods.

In Blean Forest, which then extended for many miles in the direction of the sea, the wild-boar was still hunted, and in times more remote bears had been found within its recesses. After a brief survey of this grand woodland prospect, they once more got into motion, and were soon buried amid dusky groves.

On emerging from the forest at Harbledown, they beheld the ancient city of Canterbury, with its ramparts, towers, gates, churches, and other edifices, overtopped by the noble cathedral, about a mile distant. This space being soon cleared, they crossed a bridge over a branch of the river Stour, and passing through the West-gate, a strong and stately structure flanked by two round towers, and defended by a portcullis, entered a long street bordered on either side by old and picturesque habitations.

VI.

HOW JACK AND TOM WERE VISITED BY MASTER LAUNCELOT STODMARSH, MAYOR OF CANTERBURY.

IT was now not far from noon, and the travellers, having ridden upwards of fifty miles, began to feel that they stood in need of some rest and refreshment. Accordingly, they alighted at an inn bearing as its sign a grotesque portrait of King James, which made both Jack and Tom smile as they regarded it, and, being shown into a chamber by the obsequious host, Christopher Chislet, inquired what eatables he had in the house.

"I can give your honours some rare trout from

Fordwich," returned Chislet. " Our Fordwich trout are accounted the finest in England, and such as come not even to the king's table, Heaven bless him! Then you can have a famous shield of brawn, a quarter of a kid, and a chine of beef; and, while you are discussing these, I will prepare you a dish of wild-fowl, or plovers—our plovers are dainty birds, and more toothsome than snipe or woodcock."

" The trout, the chine, and the plovers will suffice," said Tom. " And now, what wines hast thou in thy cellar? "

" Good store, and of the best, an please your honour," responded Chislet. " I have Rhenish and Gascoigne, white wine of Gaillac, and red wine of Bordeaux. Or shall I brew you a pottle of sack, or bring you a flagon of our old Kentish ale? The ale is wondrous strong and bright. I warrant you you shall taste the hops in it."

" I will take thy word for it, mine host," re-turned Tom; " but we care not for ale, however strong and well hopped. Give us a flask or two of Gaillac, if it be good, and brew a pottle of sack."

"Your honour shall be well contented," said the host.

While the repast was being prepared, Jack and Tom strolled forth to view the cathedral. Being familiar with its internal beauties, they contented themselves with a survey of the exterior, and returned just at the moment that the Fordwich trout were placed upon the table by the host. The repast was thoroughly enjoyed by the travellers, whose long ride had wonderfully sharpened their appetites.

"I never fared better than I have done to-day," observed Jack. "But we must not loiter; so call for the reckoning, Dick, and order the post-horses."

On this, Graham arose and was about to summon the host, when the latter suddenly entered, and, with a look of consternation depicted on his features, cried out:

" His worship the mayor, Master Launcelot Stodmarsh, desires to speak with you, gentlemen."

At the words, a large portly-looking man, with a very red face, strutted into the room. The mayor was followed by two functionaries bearing halberds, who placed themselves one on either side of the door, and was accompanied by Martin and the two officers from Gravesend.

On the entrance of the mayor, Jack and Tom thought it necessary to rise and salute him, and they did so with so much dignity, that the worshipful gentleman began to feel that he was in the presence of persons of importance.

" To what cause are we to attribute the honour of this visit, Mr. Mayor?" demanded Tom. " We are strangers here, and have merely halted in your city on our way to Dover."

"That I understand," replied Stodmarsh, essaying to look dignified in his turn. "But you must excuse me, gentlemen, if I say that I cannot permit your departure till you have given a satisfactory account of yourselves."

"On what plea do you venture to detain us, sir?" inquired Jack, in an authoritative tone, and with a sternness that took the mayor completely aback.

As soon as he had recovered himself, he said, with some respect,

"These officers have a warrant for your arrest from the portreve of Gravesend, Master Nicholas Holbeach. It is understood that you are about to cross over to France for an unlawful purpose—to fight a duel—a mortal duel—and it is our business to prevent it."

"Tut! tut! this is idle, sir," cried Tom. "The portreve has been wholly misinformed. We have no such design. We are peaceable travellers, as you may perceive by our deportment. This is my brother, Jack Smith, and I am not likely to fight him."

"I must have proof of that assertion, sir," rejoined the mayor, "as well as of your pacific intentions, before I can allow you to proceed on your journey. Have you no document about you to prove the correctness of your statement?"

"If I had any such document, I should decline to produce it," replied Tom, haughtily.

"Then you cannot blame me if I doubt your explanation," rejoined the mayor. "These officers must take you back to Gravesend, to be dealt with as my brother magistrate, the portreve, shall deem meet."

"Hold! Mr. Mayor," cried Tom, imperiously. "Listen to me, before you commit yourself——"

"I commit myself!" exclaimed Stodmarsh, greatly offended. "I can allow no such improper language to be used to me. I look upon you as suspicious characters, and authorise your immediate arrest. Do your duty, officers."

As the men were about to advance, Graham placed himself before them, and said, "Mr. Mayor, allow me to give you a word of advice."

"Advice, sir—advice!" cried the mayor, swelling with indignation. "I would have you to know that Launcelot Stodmarsh never takes advice."

"So I should imagine, sir," replied Graham, coolly. "Nevertheless, let me beg, before anything is done which you may have cause to regret, that you will grant us a word in private."

"The request is extremely irregular, sir," rejoined Stodmarsh, calming down. "But I shall not refuse it. If you have any explanation to give, I am ready to hear it."

And he motioned the landlord and the others to withdraw, telling his own officers to guard the door outside.

The order was obeyed by all except Martin, who contrived to slip behind a piece of furniture without being perceived.

"And now, sirs," said Stodmarsh, taking a seat,

but allowing the others to remain standing, "what have you to impart to me?"

"Mr. Mayor," said Graham, approaching him, and assuming a tone and manner that could not be mistaken, and that quite confounded the person he addressed, "it is necessary that you should be made aware that you are in the presence of two of the most important persons in the kingdom—his Highness the Prince of Wales and the Lord Marquis of Buckingham."

Thunderstruck by the information, the mayor sprang to his feet, upsetting the chair on which he had been sitting, but perceiving that he still looked incredulous, the prince and Buckingham removed their false beards; whereupon, unable to doubt longer, Stodmarsh threw himself at the feet of Charles, and said, "Pardon, your highness, pardon! I ought to have recognised you and the noble marquis even when disguised."

"There is nothing to forgive, Mr. Mayor," replied Charles, raising him graciously. "It is no reproach to you that you did not recognise us. I owe you an explanation, and you shall have it. All I require from you, on your loyalty to the king my august father, is, that you keep secret what may be disclosed to you."

"Your highness may entirely rely on my discretion," rejoined Stodmarsh.

"The fact is, Mr. Mayor, since you must know the truth," interposed Buckingham, "that in my capacity of Lord High Admiral, I am proceeding to Dover to examine into the condition and discipline of the fleet in the narrow seas, and his highness the prince has deigned to accompany me in the visit. Secresy being essential to the plan, we are only attended by my equerry, Sir Richard Graham, and are travelling by post, as you perceive. Now you know all. Send back those officers who have come on a fool's errand from Gravesend, and facilitate our departure Do this, and we shall be perfectly content."

"It shall be done instanter, my gracious lord," replied Stodmarsh, hastening towards the door.

"Hold a moment, while we put on our beards," said Buckingham, as he and the prince resumed their disguises.

This done, the mayor opened the door, and called out, "Ho, there! ho! landlord, I say! Bring out horses without delay for these gentlemen. They have perfectly satisfied me. You constables from Gravesend," he added to the two officers, " can return as you came. Tell the portreve he has been misinformed. Post-horses forthwith for Dover, I say, landlord."

"And the reckoning, let us have that, mine host," added Graham.

As soon as the room was cleared, Martin came out of his hiding-place.

"A pretty discovery I have made," he mentally ejaculated. "The prince and Buckingham! Who would have thought it? This shall to my master."

And, taking out his tablets, he traced a few lines, tore out the leaf, and folded it up.

He then went forth, and found the travellers mounting their horses. Jack was bidding adieu to the mayor, who was respectfully holding his stirrup, much to the host's astonishment. In another moment the party rode out of the courtyard, followed by a postboy with the baggage.

As soon as they were gone, the host observed to the mayor, "Will your worship acquaint me with the names of my guests?"

"Not now—not now, Master Chislet," replied Stodmarsh, mysteriously. "I am not at liberty to speak, but this I may say to you, your house has been highly honoured—most highly honoured."

"I judged as much," returned the host.

Meanwhile, Martin had taken aside one of the officers from Gravesend, and giving him the note he had prepared, desired him to deliver it on his return to the French ambassador.

"His excellency will reward you liberally—most

liberally," he added; "but here is an earnest," slipping a piece of gold into the constable's hands. "Tell him I am going to Dover, and will report further."

With this he ordered a post-horse, and rode after the travellers.

VII.

HOW JACK AND TOM WERE LODGED FOR THE NIGHT IN DOVER CASTLE.

NOTHING particular happened to Jack and Tom till they reached Barham Downs, when they left the road to examine a Roman camp, and while Tom was scrambling down the outer fosse of the earthwork, his horse slipped and threw him. Tom rose next moment without assistance, and none the worse for the fall, but the horse had sprained his shoulder, and could only limp along. Owing to this accident, the progress of the party became necessarily slow, and before they regained the highway, they observed another traveller speeding along in the direction of Dover. They shouted out to him to stop, but though he evidently heard the call, as he looked towards them, he paid no heed to the summons, but rather appeared to accelerate his pace.

"That is one of the men who followed us from Gad's Hill," observed Graham. "I saw him in the court-yard of the inn when we left Canterbury. Why is he riding so fast to Dover? Can he have obtained any information of our project? Shall I ride after him?"

"To what end?" rejoined Jack. "Even if you could overtake him, which is unlikely, you could not stay him. But I feel no sort of uneasiness. It is impossible he can have made any discovery."

"I hope not," returned Graham; "but it looks like it."

The prince now quitted his companions for a short time, and took a solitary gallop over the downs, pausing ever and anon to look around.

Little did he dream that some two years later, on the wild waste over which he was careering, a tent would be pitched, wherein his bride (*not* the bride of whom he was in quest, but Henrietta Maria of France) would first receive her court ladies.

After tracking a long valley, hemmed in on either side by lofty chalk ridges, between which ran the little river Dour, the travellers at last came in·sight of Dover, with its proud castle crowning the hill on the left.

At this juncture they perceived two horsemen riding towards them, who proved to be Sir Francis Cottington and Endymion Porter.

"Heaven save your highness, and you, my good lord," said Cottington, as he came up with Endymion Porter. "You have made good speed. We thought to meet you on Barham Downs."

"We lamed a horse, or we should have been here an hour ago," returned Charles. "But pray be covered, gentlemen. No ceremony now. Remember that I am only to be addressed as Master Jack Smith, and that this," pointing to Buckingham, "is my brother Tom. But let us hear what you have done."

"I have carried out all the instructions given me," replied Cottington. "I have hired a swift-sailing schooner, the *Fair Maid of Kent*, which, if I be not deceived in her, will convey you speedily to Boulogne; but though she is ready to sail at once, I advise you to delay your departure for a few hours. A strong wind is blowing, and there is a rough sea, but the captain of the schooner, Master Pynchen, feels sure the weather will improve, and he counsels us to wait till morning."

Though he was all impatience to cross, Charles assented to the delay.

On entering the town, the prince and his companions proceeded to an inn, where chambers had been engaged. He did not, however, remain long in-doors, but repaired with his attendants to the harbour, in order to look at the little vessel destined to convey him to the opposite shores. As Cottington had stated, it was blowing hard, and there was evidently a strong sea outside, but the *Fair Maid of Kent* was lying snugly within the port, and her appearance perfectly satisfied both Jack and Tom as to her sea-going qualifications.

While they were examining the little vessel, and debating whether they should go on board her, a party of mounted carabiniers issued from a side-street, and rode towards them across the wharf. At the head of this troop was an officer, whom the prince and his companions immediately recognised as Sir Harry Mainwaring, lieutenant of Dover Castle. They also noted that with Sir Harry was the person who had followed them from Gad's Hill to Canterbury, and had passed them on Barham Downs.

On nearing the party, Sir Harry Mainwaring, a stout, handsome man of military deportment, with a grey beard and moustaches, contrasting strongly with his bronzed visage, ordered his men to halt, and then dismounting, left his steed in charge of an equerry. Before advancing towards the party, he ordered two of the troopers to keep off all bystanders, and having seen this done, he marched towards Charles and Buckingham, saluted them, and was about to speak, when Buckingham interposed.

"Sir Harry Mainwaring," said the marquis, "it would be useless in the prince and myself to attempt disguise with you, but it is his highness's desire, and, indeed, command, that you do not allow any look or action to betray your knowledge of his person."

"I obey," replied the lieutenant, "but I fear that his highness's incognito, and your own, my lord, cannot be preserved, since you are both known to the emissary of the French ambassador, who has ridden on to apprise me of your visit. He has contrived to distance you by an hour."

"How came the man to penetrate our secret?" demanded Charles, bending his brow.

"He was present, though unobserved, during your interview with the Mayor of Canterbury," replied Mainwaring. "On the man's arrival at Dover, he rode up at once to the castle, and gave information to me. I did not entirely credit his statement, but immediately came down to satisfy myself, and I now find he spoke truth. Still, I can scarcely believe that the motive he assigned for your visit is correct."

"I know not what he has told you, Sir Harry," returned Charles, "but you shall learn the exact truth. I am proceeding to Madrid, attended by the Marquis of Buckingham and these three gentlemen."

"How? to Madrid with only these attendants!" exclaimed Mainwaring, astounded. "Your highness will forgive me if I cannot repress my astonishment."

"It is even as I have said, Sir Harry," rejoined

Charles. "I am going to Madrid on a special errand—nay, there shall be no mystery with you—I am going to fetch the Infanta. I desire to preserve the strictest incognito, and it is of the last importance that no message be sent over to France, as I would not be known during my journey through that kingdom. To-night I purpose to remain at Dover, and I shall sail for Boulogne at an early hour to-morrow, in yon little schooner.' I count upon your aid, good Sir Harry."

"I am sorry your highness has confided the project to me," returned Mainwaring, with some hesitation. "I fear it is inconsistent with my duty to allow your departure from the kingdom. Indeed, I dare not permit it."

"'Sdeath! sir, is this language to hold to your prince?" cried Buckingham, in a fury. "You will stay us at your peril, sir. You forget that I am Constable of Dover Castle, and that you are my subordinate officer."

"No, I do not forget it, my lord," replied Main-waring, respectfully. "I am ready to obey all your lawful commands. But I have a duty to perform to my sovereign and the state, which is paramount to all other considerations. I will despatch a messenger to Whitehall to ascertain his majesty's pleasure, but, till the man's return, I dare not permit his highness's departure."

"Is it not enough that the prince has vouch-safed to inform you of his intentions?" demanded Buckingham.

"No, my lord," replied Mainwaring, firmly. "For aught I know, the prince may be leaving without his royal father's sanction—nay, contrary to his injunctions."

"By Heaven, this passes all endurance!" cried Buckingham. "But it is idle to reason with one so obstinate and dull-witted. We will go in spite of you."

"No vessel shall quit this harbour till I have the king's warrant for its departure. I will take thus much upon myself, be the consequences what they may," rejoined Mainwaring, in a determined tone.

"Nay, Sir Harry is in the right," observed Charles. "You shall not need to send to Whitehall for my royal father's warrant, sir," he added to the lieutenant. "I have it with me, and will show it you."

"Enough," replied Mainwaring. "With that assurance I am perfectly content, and am ready to obey your behests. Will it please your highness, and you, my good lord, together with those with you, to lodge within the castle to-night? You will be accommodated more suitably than at an inn, and will be secure from all chance of further interruption."

To this proposition Charles readily agreed, whereupon Sir Harry besought him to mount his steed and ride to the castle; but the prince declined the offer, preferring to proceed thither on foot. Mainwaring then despatched a couple of troopers to the inn for the travellers' baggage, and calling his equerry to him, bade him take back Martin to the castle.

"I will give further orders concerning him when I arrive there," added the lieutenant, "but, meantime, do not allow him to hold communication with any one. These gentlemen," he added, "will be my guests for the night. See that lodgings are prepared for them in the Constable's Tower and in Peverell's Tower."

The equerry bowed, and, in obedience to the order he had received, rode off with the troop, taking Martin with him, who thus found himself a prisoner.

Shortly afterwards, Charles and all those with him quitted the quay, and took the road leading to the Castle Hill.

Arrived at the foot of the eminence, they commenced the ascent by tracking a zig-zag path, which conducted them to a steep flight of steps, and scaling these, they found themselves within a short distance of the outer gate of the fortress.

At this point, the grand old pile, aptly enough described by Matthew Paris as "the key and lock of the realm," reared itself majestically before them; its hoary walls studded with watch-towers girding the entire circumference of the hill, while its massive keep rose proudly amidst them. Charles had visited the fortress on one or two previous occasions, when he had been received with all the honours due to his exalted rank; when the royal banner had floated above the donjon-tower; when trumpets had sounded and drums had been beaten to herald his approach; when the whole garrison was drawn up in the outer court, and the road lined with the inhabitants of Dover; but never at such times had he gazed at the ancient fabric, replete with so many historical recollections, with feelings deep as those that impressed him now. Sentinels in steel cap and corslet, with pike on shoulder, were pacing to and

fro on the ramparts; other men-at-arms were stationed on the watch-towers and near the gate, but
these were the only inmates of the stronghold he
beheld. The castle wore its ordinary aspect, and,
thus beheld, gained infinitely in grandeur and
majesty.

From the castle, Charles turned to look at the
town and harbour, and was well pleased to find
that the works undertaken by his royal father for
the improvement of the pier, which, though strongly
built by Henry VIII., had become ruinous through
neglect, were making good progress.

Could he have foreseen the stupendous bulwark
which an after age was destined to produce; could
he have anticipated that the rude and unserviceable
pier then constructing would be supplanted, some
two hundred and forty years later, by a granite
wall projecting far into the sea, and capable of
withstanding the utmost fury of the waves; he
might have blushed at the insignificance and
almost inutility of the work then going on. But,

possessing no such foresight, he was well enough content, and deemed it an important achievement.

Rousing himself from the reverie into which he had fallen, he proceeded, with Mainwaring and Buckingham, who were standing near him, towards the gateway of the castle. Little aware of the importance of the personages who were entering the fortress, the guard stationed at the gate contented themselves with saluting the lieutenant, and bestowed a mere glance of curiosity at the others. Still, there was something in the look and deportment of the prince and Buckingham that excited the curiosity of these men.

The party had now entered the outer ballium, and as it was still light enough for an inspection of the fortress, Charles strolled for some time about the courts, examining the various towers on the walls—pausing before the old Roman pharos and the time-hallowed church, supposed to have been founded by King Lucius—after which he directed his course to the keep.

Entering it, and leaving Buckingham and the others in the state apartments on the third story, Charles, accompanied only by Mainwaring, mounted to the summit of a lofty turret, whence an extraordinarily fine view was commanded. It was now growing dusk, but even thus imperfectly beheld, the prospect was very striking. Across the Channel, the grey outline of the coast of France was distinguishable; the position of Calais being fixed by its lighthouse, while another pharos gleamed from Cape Grisnez, near Boulogne. Immediately below was the town, revealed by its twinkling lights, and the harbour with its shipping. Charles tried to make out the *Fair Maid of Kent*, but could not succeed in distinguishing her.

Undisturbed by the whistling wind, Charles remained for nearly a quarter of an hour on this lofty place of observation. He then descended with the lieutenant, and on repairing to the chamber where the others had been left, they were informed

by an attendant that the evening repast was served.
At this welcome intelligence, the whole party ad-
journed to the Constable's Tower, in a lower
chamber of which a substantial repast was laid out.
In compliance with the prince's injunctions, no
ceremony whatever was observed during the meal.
The whole party sat down together, and the conversation was carried on without restraint. Shortly
after supper, Charles and Buckingham, who were
somewhat fatigued by their lengthened journey,
withdrew to the chambers allotted them, and both
slept soundly till they were roused, an hour at
least before it was light, by wakeful Graham. The
rest of the party were already up, and prepared
for departure, and as soon as the prince and Buckingham had partaken of a hasty breakfast, they
quitted the castle under the escort of the lieutenant,
and followed by four stalwart troopers carrying the
baggage.

As they descended the Castle Hill on the way
to the harbour, Mainwaring informed Charles that

late at night, long after his highness had retired to rest, a messenger had brought a despatch from the king, ordering him to prohibit the departure of all vessels bound for the coast of France. "This order," he added, "I shall carry out as soon as your highness is safely off."

Captain Pynchen was anxiously awaiting his passengers, the wind being now fair, and promising a quick passage. The embarkation was speedily accomplished. Mainwaring saw the prince and Buckingham safely on board, and then wishing them a prosperous voyage, took his leave.

As the *Fair Maid of Kent* weighed anchor, and spread her sails to the favouring breeze, which promised soon to waft her and her precious freight to the shores of France, the morning gun was fired from Dover Castle.

VIII.

HOW JACK AND TOM CROSSED THE CHANNEL, AND RODE POST FROM BOULOGNE TO PARIS.

FOR some time Charles remained standing on the deck of the schooner, with his gaze fixed upon the shores from which he was rapidly receding. After running his eye along the line of lofty and precipitous chalk cliffs, extending on the right to the South Foreland, and on the left to Sandwich, he turned his regards to the old castle, nowhere beheld to such advantage as from the sea. Precisely at that moment the first beams of the sun began to gild the lofty keep, and ere long the grey walls encircling the hill, with the numerous watch-towers, the antique church, and the pharos, were lit up, until the entire fortress, which had hitherto looked cold and stern, assumed a bright and smiling aspect, which Charles was willing to construe into a favourable omen to his expedition. Not till castle and cliffs began to grow dim in the distance, did he bid a mental adieu to England.

No incident worthy of being chronicled occurred during the passage. When in mid-channel, those in the schooner caught sight of several men-of-war belonging to the fleet which Buckingham had professed he was about to inspect, but in other respects the voyage was monotonous, and appeared long and tedious to the travellers, all of whom were impatient to get across the Channel. We must not omit to mention that, immediately after their embarkation, Jack and Tom, deeming disguise no longer necessary, had laid aside their false beards.

Just at the hour of two in the afternoon they entered the harbour of Boulogne, and, after some little delay, were permitted by the officers of the port to disembark, and Charles, for the first time, set foot in France.

Cottington having concluded all arrangements with ·Captain Pynchen before landing, Jack and Tom underwent no detention on that score, but, followed by a couple of sailors carrying their baggage, proceeded to the Ecu d'Or, in the Grande Rue, where they were welcomed by a very civil landlord, who told them they were too late for the table d'hôte, but considerately added that he could speedily set an excellent dinner before them. This was agreed to, but the dinner was not served so promptly as promised, and being copious, took some time to discuss, consequently it was hard upon four o'clock before the travellers were in the saddle. Attended by two gaily-dressed postilions, wearing enormous jack-boots, and who made the quay echo with the clangour of their horns, they rode out of Boulogne, and, crossing a wooden bridge over the Liane, took the road to Montreuil, where they proposed to pass the night, and where they arrived, without accident or interruption, about seven o'clock, and took up their quarters at the Tête de Bœuf, renowned for its pâtés de becassines.

Rising betimes next morning, they were all on horseback soon after seven, and on the way to Amiens, which they determined to make the limit of that day's journey.

All the party were in high spirits. To Charles the novelty of travelling in a foreign land was exciting, and though the country through which he rode was uninteresting in a picturesque point of view, in his present frame of mind it became invested with charms such as many a really beautiful landscape had not revealed to him. Fortunately the weather was fine, and the state of the roads good, so that the travellers got on without annoyance.

A joyous company they were—as joyous and light-hearted as any that had preceded them on the same route. Whether it was change of clime and scene, or the excitement they had previously undergone, that occasioned this gaiety, none cared to inquire, being perfectly satisfied with the result. Even Sir Francis Cottington, who had been so strongly averse to the expedition, yielded to the enlivening influences, and began to view the project with a hopeful eye.

Though maintaining his habitual gravity of look, Charles at heart was as gleeful as his companions. Never had he been more entirely free from the melancholy which usually o'ershadowed him—never was the present more void of gloom—never did the future look brighter. Sometimes, in order to indulge in a fit of pleasant musing—to dwell upon the charms of his mistress—to conjure up the idea of their first interview, and his transports on beholding her—he would ride apart from the others —but he soon returned to join in their lively chat.

In this manner they advanced on their journey,

scarcely aware how much they had accomplished. After skirting the forest of Creçy, close to which the famous battle was won by Edward III., the thought of which roused the warlike spirit of Charles, and made him burn for the military renown of the Black Prince, they descended into the vale of the Somme, and traversed it till they reached Abbeville.

Here they alighted at the Hôtel de la Poste, situated near the Cathedral of St. Wolfram. At the doorway of the inn several travellers were congregated, who naturally regarded the new comers with curiosity, and speculated upon their quality. There was nothing, as we know, in the attire of any of the party to indicate their rank, and yet those who beheld them could not fail to be struck by the stately looks and deportment of Charles and Buckingham.

It chanced that among the observers on the occasion there were two gentlemen from St. Valery, who had lately been in England, and they both recognised the illustrious travellers—though almost doubting the evidence of their eyes. All the party had gone into the house with the exception of Graham, who stayed behind to pay the postilion, when one of these gentlemen, M. Marcellin, making a very polite bow, thus addressed the young equerry:

"Pray excuse me, monsieur, but I and my friend M. de Nouvion have recently been in England, and during our stay visited your famous race-course at Newmarket. While there, we had the singular satisfaction of beholding his Highness the Prince of Wales and the Lord Marquis of Buokingham. We saw them, monsieur—or perhaps I ought to say milord—sufficiently long to enable us to study their features carefully, and fix them upon our memory. You will not be surprised then, monsieur, when we declare that in two of your party, who have just gone in with the landlord, we conceive that we recognise Prince Charles and the lord marquis."

"I take what you say as a great compliment to my friends, messieurs," returned Graham, without the slightest embarrassment; "but you are mistaken. The gentlemen to whom you refer are very humble individuals—two brothers, the Messieurs Smith. They certainly bear some resemblance to the illustrious personages you have mentioned—enough, perhaps, to deceive a stranger."

"The resemblance is too striking in both instances to admit of doubt upon the point," observed M. de Nouvion. "Of course it is not for us to make a remark if the Prince of Wales and the lord marquis choose to travel incognito."

"I will speedily convince you of your error, messieurs," interrupted Graham. And stepping within the doorway, he shouted, "Hola! Jack and Tom. Come hither for a moment, I pray of you."

At this summons, Jack and Tom immediately came out of the salle à manger into which they had been ushered by the host, and Jack said, as if addressing an equal, "What do you want with us, Dick?"

"These gentlemen will have it that you are the Prince of Wales and my Lord of Buckingham," replied Graham. "Pray undeceive them, for they will not credit my denial."

"You do us too much honour, messieurs—far too much," observed Jack. "It is not, however, the first time that my brother Tom and myself have been taken for the important personages in question."

"I should think not," said M. Marcellin.

"The resemblance is rather unlucky for us," remarked Tom. "It has more than once got us into difficulties."

"I can easily imagine it," rejoined De Nouvion, sceptically. "It must be unpleasant also for the prince and the lord marquis to be mistaken, as they might be accidentally, for you and your brother M. Jack Smith. Of course you have seen my lord of Buckingham, monsieur?" he added.

"Oh yes, I have seen him," returned Tom. "We have seen both him and the prince, eh, Jack?"

"Frequently," returned Jack.

"Then you may possibly have remarked, as I did," returned M. de Nouvion, "that the marquis wears a ring on the first finger of the right hand —precisely such a ring as yours, M. Tom Smith— while the prince has a brooch, the counterpart of which fastens the cloak of your brother Jack?"

"Confound the rascal! how closely he must have observed us," whispered Tom to Jack. "Eh bien, messieurs," he added to the others, "if you persist in your belief, there is no more to be said. It would be unreasonable in my brother Jack and myself to be angry with you for so flattering an error, and, though neither of us is likely to become a marquis or a prince of the blood, we must accept the titles for the moment, since you are determined to invest us with them."

So saying, he bowed, as did Jack, and both,

laughing heartily, returned to the salle à manger, followed by Graham, and leaving M. de Nouvion and his friend in some perplexity.

It soon became apparent, from the extraordinary deference paid to Jack and Tom, that Messieurs de Nouvion and Marcellin had communicated their opinion as to the real rank of his guests to the hôtelier. With a thousand apologies, the host besought his distinguished guests to remove to a private room; but this they declined, saying they did not desire better accommodation than ordinary travellers.

"You are extremely obliging, my good host," remarked Tom, "but we know the cause of your civility, and it is proper we should set you right. Two gentlemen, with whom we have just been conversing, are under the delusion that we are grand seigneurs travelling incognito. The notion is absurd. We have not the slightest pretension to high rank, and are simply what we seem."

"That is quite possible, milord," replied the

hôtelier, bowing, "because to me you seem to be princes."

"'Sdeath! take us for what you will," cried Tom. "All we ask is, not to be charged like princes. Put nothing down for rank in your reckoning."

The host declared he would not, but failed to keep his word. The best the house could produce was set before his guests; but they had to pay handsomely for their entertainment. Their indifference to the heavy charge which he had not scrupled to make, confirmed the shrewd host in his opinion of their rank. On the departure of the travellers, the whole house assembled in the courtyard to see them mount, and bows and curtseys were made them on all sides, which they very graciously returned.

At Amiens, where they arrived before dusk, they put up at the Hôtel de France, and visited the cathedral during the solemnisation of evening mass—Charles being lost in admiration of the extraordinary architectural beauty of the interior of this noble Gothic pile.

Next morning they started at an early hour for Paris, and did not loiter on their journey. With no little satisfaction they found themselves at Saint Denis, where they changed horses for the last time. A short stage brought them to the faubourgs of Paris, and they entered the city by the Porte Saint Denis—not the existing triumphal arch, but an older portal, built by Charles IX.

On passing through the gateway, Charles experienced that emotion which every stranger must feel on first beholding a city of which he has heard much and longed to visit. All was new to him— habitations, people, costumes—and he gazed around with insatiable curiosity. His course led him through the Rue Saint Denis, and its old and picturesque houses delighted him, but it was on reaching the quays on the banks of the Seine, and while crossing the Pont-Neuf, that Paris was displayed to him in all its marvellous beauty. Notre-

Dame, the Châtelet, the Louvre, the Tuileries, and a multitude of less important structures, then burst upon his gaze, filling him with admiration. But he had no time to dwell on the picture. Passing the Collége de Quatre Nations, and along the Quai des Theatins, the party soon reached the Rue de Bourbon, and alighted at the Hôtel des Etrangers.

IX.

HOW JACK AND TOM WERE GRACIOUSLY RECEIVED BY THE DUC DE MONTBAZON.

In the course of the evening Graham brought word that some brilliant fêtes were just then taking place at court, whereupon Jack expressed a strong desire to be present at one of them on the following day. Tom declared he saw no difficulty in the matter, and undertook to obtain admission to the Louvre. However, as they were unprovided with fitting attire, a messenger was at once despatched to M. Marolles, the court tailor, who presently repaired to the hotel, and received an order for three magnificent suits. Marolles not only undertook to furnish these habiliments at an early hour on the morrow, but to provide the three gentlemen with all else they might require to make a befitting appearance at the royal fête. Moreover, he promised to bring M. Gaston, the court perruquier, with a good choice of periwigs à la mode de la cour. This important matter arranged, Jack and Tom retired to recruit themselves after the fatigues of the day, and prepare for the festivities of the morrow.

When they arose next morning, they found Marolles and Gaston in attendance. Their dresses became them to admiration—at least, Marolles declared so—and Gaston was quite satisfied with the sit of their perukes—the latter, it may be mentioned in passing, had been ordered in some degree to disguise their features.

At a later hour in the morning, arrayed in their splendid habiliments, and wearing their flowing perukes, Jack and Tom, attended by Graham, who was equally richly attired, drove in a coach to the Louvre, and were set down in the great court.

On entering the palace, their distinguished appearance satisfied the ushers that they were persons of importance, and they were at once admitted to the cabinet of the Duc de Montbazon, grand chamberlain to the queen, by whom the royal fêtes were superintended. The duke, who was a very formal personage, received them with ceremonious politeness. They were presented to him as the Messieurs Smith, three Englishmen who were passing through Paris to Madrid, and they noticed that the duke smiled slightly when this announcement was made.

"We are quite aware, M. le Duc," said Tom, "that we ought to have been presented to you by our ambassador, but as time presses, and we have only a single day in Paris, we have ventured to come direct to you, being inflamed with a most ardent desire to witness the royal fête, which we are told is to be given this evening."

"I will do all in my power to oblige you, messieurs," returned Montbazon, in the most gracious manner possible. "To-day, as you may possibly be aware, a grand banquet is given by the queen-mother, Marie de Médicis, to his majesty and the principal persons of the court. The banquet will be followed by a superb allegorical ballet, which will take place in the grand salle de danse; and in this ballet, besides the fairest of the court dames, the Princess Henriette Marie and my gracious mistress, our lovely young queen, will dance."

"It is chiefly to behold your young queen, Anne of Austria, of whose beauty we have heard such ravishing descriptions, that we desire to witness this ballet, M. le Duc," remarked Jack.

"I need scarcely tell you, messieurs," said Montbazon, "that, as conductor of the royal fêtes, I have been compelled to refuse a vast number of applications from members—some of them distinguished members—of the court to be present at this ballet, but I am disposed to make an exception in your favour. As strangers, the king will feel that you have a greater claim upon his hospitality than his own subjects possess. In his majesty's name, therefore, I invite you, messieurs, to the banquet, and to the ballet."

"You overwhelm us with obligation, M. le Duc," replied Jack. "Gratified as we are by the invitation, we can scarcely accept it, as we feel that you are straining courtesy too far."

"Nay, do not stand on ceremony, messieurs," replied Montbazon. "I should be very sorry that you missed these fêtes, and as your stay in Paris is limited to a single day, you cannot have another opportunity. I myself will see you well placed."

"We have no rank to entitle us to any but the lowest place," observed Tom. "Indeed, we ought not to sit down among the court nobility."

A singular smile played upon the duke's countenance, and he said, with some significance, "Be assured I will assign you proper places, messieurs."

Just then an usher entered, and informed the

grand chamberlain that the English ambassador was without, and craved an audience.

"This is lucky!" exclaimed Montbazon. "It will spare you the necessity of waiting upon Sir Edward Herbert."

"One word, M. le Duc," said Jack. "I must pray you not to admit him."

"Not admit him!" cried the duke, feigning surprise. "Wherefore not?"

"You shall know as soon as we are alone," rejoined the other.

"Entreat his excellency to excuse me for a moment," said Montbazon to the usher. "I shall soon be disengaged."

"It is right, M. le Duc," said Charles, as soon as they were alone, "that you should know who we are; but in making the disclosure, I must throw myself upon your generosity to keep the matter secret."

"It is perfectly safe in my hands, prince," replied Montbazon, rising and bowing profoundly "I knew you and my lord of Buckingham the moment you entered. Marolles informed me you had sent for him, and I was, therefore, prepared for this visit. You look surprised, but I received information of your arrival in Paris last night from the lieutenant-general of police, to whom it was communicated."

"Is the king aware of my arrival?" inquired Charles.

"Not as yet," replied the duke. "I intended to apprise him, but if it is really your highness's desire to pass through Paris without a public appearance at court, I will not mention the matter to his majesty till after your departure."

"You will do me an immense favour, for which I shall ever feel grateful, M. le Duc," rejoined Charles. "If presented to his majesty, I must tarry here for some days, and I am bound on an expedition of the utmost urgency——"

"To Spain," remarked Montbazon, with a smile. "I understand. Your highness may rest easy, I will not thwart your project, but will facilitate your departure. Your ambassador is in the ante-chamber, and will be sure to see you as you go out. Let me beg of you, therefore, to pass forth this way."

So saying, he opened a side-door communicating with a private staircase, through which Charles and his companions, with a renewed expression of their gratitude, made an exit.

X.

HOW JACK AND TOM DROVE ABOUT PARIS, AND WHAT THEY SAW DURING THE DRIVE.

DETERMINED to make the most of their time, Charles and his companions spent several hours in driving about Paris, noting every object of interest that came under their observation,—palaces, hotels of the nobility, ancient habitations, theatres, churches, fortresses, prisons, hospitals, colleges, bridges, and public edifices of all kinds. They tracked the Rue Saint Honoré and the Rue Saint Antoine from end to end, visited a multitude of churches and convents by the way, strolled about the Place Royale, and spent some time in contemplating the Bastille. Surrounded by a deep moat, approached only by a drawbridge, bristling with ordnance, and flanked by towers, this terrible state prison and fortress seemed almost a counterpart of the Tower of London, though it wanted the majesty of the latter structure.

" 'Tis a stern and sullen pile, the Bastille," observed Charles, " and the heart aches when one thinks of the multitude of captives confined within it."

" Louis XIII. would say the same thing of the Tower, if he chanced to behold it," rejoined Buckingham.

" Possibly he might," remarked Charles, gloomily. " And yet the Tower never affected me so profoundly."

" And no doubt his most Christian Majesty makes light of the Bastille," said Buckingham, " and thinks it the finest building in his fair city of Paris, as it certainly is the most useful. Where else could he safely lodge so many state offenders, and prevent them from uttering a complaint? Would to Heaven it were as easy for our dear dad and gossip to send a traitor to the Tower as it is for Louis to incarcerate one in the Bastille! The lettre de cachet is an admirable invention. No accusation—no trial—secret arrest and secret imprisonment. With the lettre de cachet and the Bastille, a monarch or his minister may play the despot with impunity. The time may come when your highness may enjoy the truly regal privilege of the lettre de cachet."

"Any attempt to exercise such arbitrary power in England would cause a revolution," observed Charles. "But you ever jest with the most serious subjects, Tom. Let us leave this moody pile. The sight of it makes me melancholy."

"Whither shall we go?" cried Buckingham. "Yonder is the Porte Saint Antoine. Suppose

we pass through it, and drive outside the walls to
the Porte Saint Martin?   Your highness will then
have seen all Paris."

"Not quite all, Tom," returned Charles, "but
enough to convince me that it is a wondrously
beautiful city, far more picturesque than London,
and yet, I own, I like London best."

"'Twould be strange if you did not," remarked
Buckingham. "But we must embellish London,
and make it surpass Paris in beauty."

"London, in my opinion, needs no embellishment," said Graham. "The Thames is a far finer
river than the Seine; London Bridge is handsomer than the Pont Neuf; Whitehall is a nobler
palace than the Louvre; Saint Paul's surpasses
Notre-Dame in grandeur; and we are all agreed
that the Tower is infinitely more majestic than the
Bastille."

"You are right, Dick," observed Charles. "And
yet, as a whole, Paris is a finer city than London."

"I am loth to admit so much," said Graham. "But your highness is a better judge than I am, and I must needs defer to your opinion. Unquestionably, the habitations here are loftier than with us."

"And more picturesque," said Charles. "We have no street like the Rue Saint Antoine, which we have just traversed."

"None so long, I own," rejoined Graham. "But give me the Strand, or Fleet-street."

"What say you to the Samaritaine on the Pont Neuf?" demanded Buckingham.

"A mere mechanical toy," replied Graham; "quaint and pretty enough, but Saint Dunstan's clock is better worth seeing."

"Have you no admiration for the Tuileries?" said Buckingham.

"The palace is not entirely to my taste," returned Graham. "I like Saint James's better."

"You are as void of taste as you are obstinate, Dick," observed Charles, laughing. "But whatever I may think of the beauties of this city—and manifold they are—rest assured I would not exchange London for it."

While this conversation took place, they passed through the Porte Saint Antoine, and pursuing a broad road laid out on the top of the counterscarp, skirted the old walls until they came to the Porte Saint Martin, when they again entered the city, and drove direct to their hotel in the Rue de Bourbon.

While the prince and his companions were thus employing their time, Sir Francis Cottington and Endymion Porter were fully occupied in preparations for the journey to be undertaken next day. Their first business was to despatch a courier to King James, with a letter apprising his majesty of the safe arrival of the prince and Buckingham in Paris. This done, they proceeded to a banker in the Rue des Lombards, where they obtained gold for some of the bills of exchange with which they were furnished; and being thus amply provided with funds, as well for the journey as for immediate requirement, they procured, in pursuance of the orders they had received, two handsome riding-suits for the prince and Buckingham. Moreover, having suffered grievously from the neglect of due provision in this respect during their ride from Boulogne to Paris, they purchased well-padded saddles for the whole party, and took care that the holsters were furnished with pistols. Pistols also were provided for the belt, and musquetoons for the shoulder, so that henceforth the travellers would be armed to the teeth, and able, it was thought, to resist any attack by robbers that might be made on them during the journey.

"You have made due provision for our comfort as well as for our security, gentlemen," observed Charles, as he examined these articles, which were laid out for his inspection. "I am particularly glad to see these easy saddles. We could scarce have got to Madrid without them."

" And these laced riding-habits, broad-leaved

grey hats, and funnel-topped boots, will transform us into French cavaliers in a trice," cried Buckingham. "We have only to don these habiliments, and wear our moustaches en croc, and the metamorphosis will be complete."

"These riding-dresses are the counterpart of those worn by his majesty Louis XIII. while hunting, my good lord," replied Cottington.

"They are handsome enough for any monarch in Christendom," cried Buckingham. "But, thus attired, we shall be compelled to change our designation. We can be Smiths no longer."

"That must not be," returned Charles. "As John Smith I have started on the expedition, and John Smith I will continue till I reach Madrid."

"And I of course shall remain brother Tom," said Buckingham. "After all, one English name is as good as another in France, and it signifies little what we are called."

At this juncture, a servant entered to say that a messenger from the Duc de Montbazon was without, and shortly afterwards a well-dressed personago was shown into the room. He announced himself as M. Chevilly, confidential valet to the duke, and thus declared his mission:

"Highness," he said, making a profound obeisance to the prince, "I have been sent by the Duc de Montbazon to attend upon you, and upon the noble marquis, if you will deign to employ me. My master deeply regrets that he is unable personally to attend upon your highness, but he has given me ample instructions. He has charged me to say that he will send his own carriage to convey you to the Luxembourg, where the banquet given by her majesty the queen-mother takes place. If permitted, I shall have the supreme honour of attending your highness to the palace, and after the banquet will conduct you to the Louvre, where you will witness the grand ballet."

"The duke is, indeed, most considerate," said Charles. "I fear I may put him to some inconvenience."

"My master is anxious to anticipate your wishes," returned Chevilly. "If I understand aright, your highness designs to start at an early hour to-morrow morning for Spain. May I venture to ask whether any of your gentlemen have taken the trouble to order post-horses?"

"Not as yet," returned Cottington. "We await his highness's orders. But there can be no difficulty about the matter."

"Pardon me, monseigneur," said Chevilly. "There is great difficulty, as you would have found, had you made application. Without my master's intervention you would have had no post-horses."

"The deuce!" exclaimed Buckingham. "That would have been awkward. But why should we be refused?"

"Because the lieutenant-general of police had interdicted your departure till his majesty's pleasure respecting you should be ascertained, my lord," rejoined Chevilly. "My master, however, has made it his business to remove the obstacle, and, I rejoice to say, has succeeded. Here is an order for the horses, countersigned by the head of the police," he added, delivering it to Cottington. "You can start at any hour you deem proper."

"Another great obligation I am under to the duke," observed Charles.

"A mere trifle," said Chevilly. "In an hour the carriage will be here to convey you to the Luxembourg. I will await your highness's further orders without."

And with a profound bow he withdrew.

Shortly afterwards, Charles, with Buckingham and Graham, retired to their respective chambers, and proceeded to make their toilettes with great care.

XI.

HOW JACK AND TOM DINED AT THE LUXEMBOURG; AND HOW
THEY WERE PRESENTED TO QUEEN MARIE DE MEDICIS.

PUNCTUALLY at the time appointed, the magnificent equipage belonging to the Duc de Montbazon entered the court-yard of the hotel, and Charles, with Buckingham and Graham, being ceremoniously conducted to it by Chevilly, were driven to the Luxembourg. Chevilly went with them, posted on the marche-pied.

The palace of the Luxembourg—still one of the chief ornaments of the French capital—was at this time in all its freshness and splendour, having only been completed a few years previously by Marie de Médicis, who spent an enormous sum upon its construction, and in its internal embellishment. Modelled upon the Palazzo Pitti at Florence, it possessed charming gardens laid out in the Italian style, and ornamented with marble fountains and statues.

On arriving at the palace, the carriage containing Charles and his companions passed through the gateway into the grand court, which was filled at the time with splendid equipages. On alighting, our travellers entered a spacious vestibule, thronged with gentlemen ushers, pages, valets, and musketeers of the royal guard. Here they were met by Chevilly, who preceded them up a noble staircase, and led them along a magnificent corridor, adorned with antique statues and paintings by the first Italian masters.

Eventually, the party were ushered into a large and gorgeously furnished room, in which were assembled the guests. The company, as may be supposed, consisted of the élite of the French nobility, and they were all as much distinguished by aristocratic deportment and refinement of manner as by splendour of apparel.

Montbazon had taken care to make it known that three Englishmen had been invited to the banquet, and when Charles and his companions made their appearance, it was at once understood they must be the persons referred to by the duke. But who were they? This was a question that no one could answer, and Montbazon not being present at the moment, the general curiosity remained unsatisfied. That they were persons of high rank none doubted, but no one—not even the ushers—had heard their titles.

Meanwhile, Charles and his companions, not unconscious of the curiosity they excited, and secretly amused by it, had halted, and remained standing at some little distance from the rest of the company. The remarkable dignity of the prince's deportment, and the noble character of his features, drew all eyes towards him, while Buckingham's stately figure and haughty manner made him also a mark for general observation. There were some fair observers, however, who thought Sir Richard Graham the handsomest of the three.

Charles seemed perfectly indifferent to the effect which he produced upon the assemblage, and though he did not assume any air of superiority, it was impossible that he could disguise his habitual majesty of deportment. Buckingham, accustomed to outshine all the members of his own court by the splendour of his apparel and the magnificence of his ornaments, was mortified to find himself eclipsed by several of the nobles on the present occasion, and lamented the want of his diamond girdle and ropes of pearls. He looked around proudly, as was his wont at Whitehall, and offended some of the high-spirited young nobles by his supercilious air.

His haughty glance was still ranging over the

courtly throng, when large folding-doors at the upper end of the room were thrown open, and a gentleman usher, attended by a number of pages dressed in white satin, announced their majesties the king and queen.

Preceded by the Duc de Montbazon, bearing his wand of office, and walking backwards, the young monarch then came forth, leading the queen-mother by the hand. Louis XIII. was of slight figure, but well proportioned, with handsome features and fine eyes. His pourpoint and mantle were of crimson damask, embroidered with gold and enriched with precious stones, and round his neck he wore a chain with the order of the Toison d'Or. His majesty seemed out of health. He walked feebly, and his countenance bore traces of suffering.

Marie de Médicis, who still retained much of her beauty, had set off her noble person to the utmost advantage. The stomacher of her dark satin dress blazed with diamonds and rubies. A carcanet of pearls encircled her still snowy throat, and wreaths of pearls adorned her tresses, which had lost none of their raven hue. Her eyes were lustrous, her brow smooth as marble, and her carriage majestic and imperious.

On the appearance of the royal party, the company immediately drew aside to allow them passage, and profound reverences were made on all sides. These were very graciously acknowledged by the queen-mother, and somewhat coldly by her royal son, who scarcely deigned to look around.

Charles and his companions escaped the king's notice, but not that of Marie de Médicis, who appeared much struck by their appearance, and vouchsafed them a gracious smile. Little did Louis XIII. deem that within a few paces of him stood the heir to the throne of a kingdom powerful as his own—a prince with whom he was destined to be allied—or he might have bestowed something more than a heedless glance upon him.

However, though both were objects of interest to him, it was neither with the king nor the queen-mother that Charles was now occupied. His attention was engrossed by the lovely young queen who followed them. Anne of Austria was then about twenty-four, and consequently in the full éclat of her beauty. Her figure was exquisite, and her movements combined Castilian dignity with Andalusian grace. In stature she was somewhat below the ordinary female standard, but this circumstance detracted nothing from the effect she produced. Her feet and hands were the smallest and most beautiful imaginable, and her waist taper, yet admirably rounded. Her features, lovely in expression as in form, were lighted up by large dark eyes beaming with mingled fire and tenderness. Her nose was small, and, judged by classic rule, might have been termed too flat, but it was charming nevertheless, as was her little mouth, the under lip of which protruded beyond its roseate partner, proclaiming her a true daughter of the house of Austria. Her rich brown locks were wreathed with diamonds, and gathered in crisp little curls, as was then the mode, upon her white open brow. Her dress was of yellow damask, the body being covered with twisted fringes of diamonds and precious stones. In her right hand she carried a Spanish fan, and her left hand was accorded to Cardinal Richelieu, who had the honour of conducting her to the banquet.

The wondrous beauty of the young queen transcended any ideas that Charles and Buckingham had formed of it, and the latter was perfectly dazzled, her charms kindling an instantaneous flame in his breast.

On her part, Anne of Austria had remarked both Buckingham and the prince, and she was not unconscious of the ardent glance of admiration which the former had dared to fix upon her. But for this glance, which called the blood to her cheek, she might have drawn Richelieu's attention to the strangers, and inquired their names.

"How lovely the queen is," whispered Charles to his favourite.

"She is perfection," rejoined Buckingham; "and if the Infanta Maria is only equally lovely, as I doubt not she must be, your highness will be the happiest of men."

"Fair as the queen is, they say Louis is insensible to her charms, and neglects her for Madame de Chevreuse," remarked Charles. "Looking on her, I cannot believe the scandal."

"If she be so neglected," rejoined Buckingham, breathing hard, "his majesty merits the fate of a careless husband. But see! who comes next? One need not be told that it is the Princess Henriette Marie. Her beauty pales beside that of Anne of Austria."

"Hum! I am not sure of that," rejoined Charles. "They are different in style, but both are beautiful."

The fair young princess, who was now led past them by the Duc de Guise, was not yet fifteen, and consequently her personal charms could not be fully developed. But there was the promise of extraordinary beauty about her; and her magnificent black eyes, luxuriant black tresses, dark glowing cheeks, coral lips, and pearly teeth, showed what her charms would be when arrived at maturity. Henriette Marie inherited all her mother's beauty, and, indeed, was so like her mother, that, at Florence, she might have passed for a daughter of the house of Médicis.

As the princess moved gracefully along under the conduct, as we have said, of the Duc de Guise, her eyes encountered those of Charles, which were fixed upon her. There was nothing to alarm her, as there had been in Buckingham's bold gaze at the queen, but there was something in the look that vibrated to her heart, and awakened an emotion such as she had never previously experienced. A kind of fascination was exercised over her, and she could not withdraw her gaze from the dark handsome countenance that enthralled it. A strange presentiment crossed her, and seemed to announce that her future fate was in some way connected with the person she beheld.

"That gentleman must be a stranger," she remarked, in a low voice, to the Duc de Guise. "I do not remember to have seen him before."

"I know not who he is," replied the duke, regarding Charles with surprise. "But I will inquire anon, and inform you."

Charles's eyes followed the princess as she glided gracefully along, and it would almost seem that she felt their influence, for she turned her head slightly, and bestowed a second glance upon him.

"A merveille!" exclaimed Buckingham. "You have evidently created an interest in the bosom of the fair Henriette Marie, and if a corresponding impression has been produced upon your highness, we had better stay where we are, instead of prosecuting our journey to Madrid."

" Pshaw!" exclaimed Charles. " The princess is very beautiful, I admit—very captivating—but I cannot swerve from my allegiance to the Infanta. I begin to think we have run great hazard of [discovery in attending this banquet. Many inquiring looks have been fixed upon us."

" Amongst others, those of the princess," replied Buckingham. " She has evidently been trying to ascertain who your highness may be, but I hope she will not learn the truth till we have left Paris, or there will be considerable risk of our detention. If she is as clever as she is beautiful, she will not let such a prize escape her. Heaven grant she display not too much interest in you to the Duc de Montbazon, or he may counter-order the post-horses."

" We were unwise to come here," observed Charles, gravely.

" That I feel," replied Buckingham. " Having lost my heart to the lovely queen, I shall be tormented evermore with a hopeless passion. But being here, we must go through with it. Retreat is now impossible."

Meanwhile the guests marched on. Next after the Princess Henriette Marie came her younger brother, Gaston de France, Duc d'Orléans, conducting Mademoiselle de Montpensier, whom he subsequently espoused..

Monsieur, as the Duc d'Orléans was styled, was presumptive heir to the throne, the king being as yet without issue by his union with Anne of Austria. Of an ambitious nature, and indisposed to wait the due course of events, Gaston was ever conspiring against his royal brother, but his designs were invariably baffled by the vigilance of Richelieu, who surrounded him with spies, and received intelligence of all his machinations.

The Duc d'Orléans was a prince of very noble presence, and looked more robust than the king, though his features were not so handsome as those of Louis XIII. He was his mother's favourite son, and as she would gladly have seen him on the throne, she secretly supported his schemes, and by so doing excited the suspicion of Richelieu and the king. Into these intrigues, however, we need not enter, as they have no relation to our story. On the present occasion Gaston was splendidly attired, and made a very magnificent appearance. Aware that he secretly aspired to the throne, Charles and Buckingham regarded him with curiosity; but they sought in vain to read his character in his looks. He was a profound dissembler, and his visage was a mask to hide his thoughts. The Duc d'Orléans and Mademoiselle de Montpensier were succeeded by a long train, comprising, as we have said, the most distinguished personages of the court, but it was not till the whole of these had passed by that Charles and his companions fell into the line. A host of pages and valets, amongst whom came Chevilly, brought up the rear.

"This flagrant violation of etiquette in your highness's case would drive Sir John Finett distracted, if he were to hear of it. And the Duc de Montbazon must be equally annoyed," remarked Graham to the prince.

"It gives me not the slightest concern," rejoined Charles. "In reality, there is no violation of etiquette whatever, since I am only known as Jack Smith."

Passing through an ante-room lined with attendants in rich liveries, the guests were ushered into the banqueting-hall — a noble apartment, with a ceiling painted with frescoes, and walls hung with tapestry, not of sombre hue and design, but light and pleasing to the eye, representing pastoral scenes and flowers. A flourish of trumpets was sounded as the royal party entered the banqueting-chamber.

At the upper end of the table there was a dais, at which the queen-mother sat beneath a canopy of state, with the royal party on either side of her. These august personages were served only by nobles, who esteemed it a proud distinction to be so employed.

In all respects the banquet was regal. The plate was superb, the meats of the choicest kind, the wines varied and exquisite. Officers were stationed at short intervals, and numberless attendants did their duty most efficiently. Though placed among the inferior guests, and at the lower end of the board, Charles and his companions were well satisfied with their position, inasmuch as they were free from observation themselves, and had a full view of the royal party at the upper table.

Buckingham ate little, though tempted by many delicacies, but feasted his eyes on the charms of the queen, and Charles's gaze took the same direction, though, sooth to say, he looked quite as much at the Princess Henriette Marie as at Anne of Austria. Graham was by no means indifferent to the splendour of the scene, and looked frequently towards the dais, but he did not allow his curiosity to interfere with his enjoyment of the dainties set before him.

Our three travellers sat together, with the prince

in the midst, and their haughty reserve and taciturnity effectually isolated them from their neighbours, who regarded them with the dislike which Englishmen at all times have contrived to inspire among their Gallic neighbours. They were sedulously attended upon by Chevilly, who stood behind them during the repast.

Though splendid and profuse, the banquet did not occupy much more than an hour. It was terminated by a marshal, who proclaimed in a loud voice from the dais that her majesty the queen-mother drank to her guests, whereupon all the company arose and bowed towards the upper table in acknowledgment of the honour done them. After this, the royal party retired—the ceremonies observed at their departure being similar to those which had marked their entrance. The guests followed in the same order as before, and returned to the grand saloon.

On entering this room, Charles and Buckingham looked in vain for Anne of Austria and the young princess. They had already set out for the Louvre to prepare for the ballet, and the king and the rest of the royal party speedily followed them.

Marie de Médicis, however, felt constrained to stay with her guests, and it was at this juncture that the Duc de Montbazon, who had not hitherto found an opportunity of addressing the prince and his companions, approached them, and stated, with a significant smile, that her majesty the queen-mother had commanded him to present them to her.

"Her majesty has remarked [your presence, prince," he added, in a low voice, "and has made particular inquiries about your highness and my Lord of Buckingham. I told her you were the Messieurs Smith, but she would not be satisfied with that description — neither would the queen nor the Princess Henriette Marie. So I was compelled to avow the truth to them, and disclose your real rank."

"How, M. le Duc?" exclaimed Charles, with

a look of displeasure. "You promised to preserve my secret."

"It is perfectly safe with these royal ladies, prince," rejoined Montbazon. "In fact, no option was left me. Had I not confessed, discovery must infallibly have ensued. Now you are safe. It is not strange that you have escaped the king's notice, for his majesty rarely troubles himself about strangers, but it is lucky that Cardinal Richelieu did not remark you."

"Under these circumstances, M. le Duc, will it be prudent to proceed to the Louvre?" said Charles.

"I see no danger whatever, your highness," returned Montbazon; "and I may be permitted to add, that the queen and the Princess Henriette Marie will be greatly disappointed if you are not present at the ballet. I told them of the ardent desire you had evinced to behold it."

"It would be inconsistent with your highness's

chivalrous character to retire now," observed Buckingham.

"After what the Duc de Montbazon has just said, I should never dream of retiring," rejoined Charles.

"I am delighted to hear it," said Montbazon. "Chevilly shall place masks in the carriage, and you can wear them in the ball-room, so there will be small chance of discovery. But now allow me to conduct you to her majesty."

Marie de Médicis was seated on a fauteuil, surrounded by a number of lords and ladies, but as Montbazon approached, she motioned her entourage to withdraw, and most graciously received the prince and his companions on their presentation.

"I was little aware whom I had the honour of entertaining, prince," she observed to Charles; "but I need not say how much indebted I am to the Duc de Montbazon for enabling me to exercise some slight hospitality towards your highness and the Marquis of Buckingham. I am sorry your stay in Paris is so short, but I presume there is more attraction in Madrid, whither I understand you are going."

"I have found Paris so charming, that I greatly regret leaving it, madame," replied Charles. "And my regrets will not be diminished by the glimpse I have been permitted to enjoy of your brilliant court."

"It is your own fault, prince, that you are restricted to a mere glimpse," rejoined Marie de Médicis. "Can I not offer you sufficient temptation to remain here?—if but for a week. Will you not delay your journey to Madrid for that time?"

"Impossible, madame," replied Charles. "Feeling I can place confidence in your majesty, I will at once own that secresy and despatch are indispensable to the success of the expedition I have undertaken. I ought not to be here this evening, but I could not resist the desire to behold your court, and the Duc de Montbazon kindly consented to gratify me."

"Montbazon did well," rejoined Marie de Médicis. "Since you are resolved to go, prince, I shall not press you further. Doubtless you are engaged on some romantic enterprise," she added, with a smile; "and I would not, on any account, interfere with it. You are said to be the most chivalrous prince in Europe, and the hazardous journey you have undertaken proves you deserve the title. What shall I say of you, my Lord of Buckingham, except that you are a worthy companion of the prince?"

"I am afraid your majesty will look upon us as two crazy knight-errants," rejoined Buckingham. "Since I have had the honour to be your guest, I have been so enchanted with what I have seen, that I begin to view our expedition in a different light, and should not be sorry if you could induce his highness to forego it."

"I fear the attempt would be fruitless," said Marie de Médicis; "but perhaps the prince may change his mind before the end of the evening. I am now going to the Louvre, and shall expect to see you there at the ballet. Au revoir."

On this, Charles and his companions retired, and the queen-mother arising, with a gracious salutation to those around her quitted the apartment, attended by her ladies of honour and by the Duc de Montbazon, and entered her carriage.

Her guests followed her example, and in less than an hour the whole of the company were transferred from the palace of the Luxembourg to that of the Louvre.

XII.

HOW JACK AND TOM WITNESSED A GRAND BALLET AT THE LOUVRE; AND HOW TOM DANCED A SARABAND WITH ANNE OF AUSTRIA, AND JACK DANCED THE PAVANE WITH THE PRINCESS HENRIETTE MARIE.

ACCUSTOMED as they were to pomp and splendour, and familiar with every possible display of regal magnificence, it was not without admiration almost amounting to wonder that Charles and his companions passed through the gorgeous halls of the Louvre, now brilliantly illuminated, and filled with richly-attired guests.

On this occasion the superb suite of apartments, surpassing in size and splendour those of any other palace, were thrown open, and at no time had a more numerous or a more distinguished assemblage been collected within them. All that the court of France, then the most elegant and refined as well as the most aristocratic in Europe, could boast in the way of nobility and high birth, was present. The chief beauties and the most accomplished gallants belonging to a court maintained by a young king and a lovely queen were at the Louvre that night, and Charles and Buckingham were free to admit that they had never seen so many charming dames and noble-looking cavaliers as were now met together. Something of this effect might be owing to the gorgeous dresses, and Buckingham more than ever regretted the want of his own splendid habiliments and diamonds.

Moving on with the glittering stream, Charles and his companions passed through many gorgeous rooms, until they reached a noble hall called the "Salle Neuve de la Reine." At the doors of this grand saloon, in which the ballet was about to take place, numerous gentlemen ushers and pages were stationed, and before entering it the prince and his companions put on their masks.

Anne of Austria, like most of her country-women, was passionately fond of dancing, and excelled in the art, and the king, though caring little for the amusement, was willing to gratify her tastes. Balls and masquerades, therefore, were of frequent occurrence at the Louvre, greatly to the delight of the younger members of the court.

The Salle Neuve de la Reine, in which these entertainments usually took place, was a spacious and lofty apartment, admirably adapted to the pur-pose, as it allowed ample space for the movements of a vast number of couples. The panels were covered with sky-blue satin, and the numerous mirrors were festooned with flowers. At one side there was an orchestra, filled by the best musicians from the Grand Opera. Viewed from the doors by which the company entered, this splendid saloon presented the most charming coup d'œil imaginable. The atmosphere was loaded with perfumes, which almost intoxicated the senses. At the upper end of the room was a canopy, beneath which, on raised fauteuils, sat Marie de Médicis, Anne of Austria, and the Princess Henriette Marie, surrounded by a bevy of court dames, but neither the king nor Monsieur, nor any other grand seigneur, except the Duc de Montbazon, stood near them.

Just as Charles and his companions entered the saloon, the grand allegorical ballet was about to commence. A lively prelude was played by the orchestra, and, at its close, the side-doors communicating with another apartment flew open, and a band of Olympian divinities, attended by minstrels clashing cymbals, and playing on the lyre and the lute, swept into the hall, and taking up a position in its centre, proceeded to execute a classic dance. Personated by some of the loveliest dames and damsels of the court, and robed in gauzy drapery that displayed their symmetry of limb to perfection, these goddesses ravished the hearts of the beholders, and Juno, Pallas, and Venus looked *so* lovely, that Buckingham declared he should be as much puzzled as Paris himself if called upon to decide which was the fairest.

Besides the principal dancers, there was a numerous corps de ballet, composed of nymphs, shepherds, and fauns, and this troop mingled with the dance at intervals, and heightened its effect. The grace and beauty of the performers in the ballet would have sufficed to ensure its success; but it was admirably contrived, and presented a series of exquisite classical pictures. The group with which the dance closed was charmingly conceived, and formed so enchanting a picture, that the spectators were transported with delight, and could scarcely repress their enthusiasm. As it was, a murmur of admiration pervaded the assemblage.

When this charming picture was broken up, Juno, accompanied by the two other goddesses, stepped towards the seats occupied by Marie de

Médicis and Anne of Austria, and bending before their majesties, thus addressed them:

> Je ne suis plus cette Junon
> Pleine de gloire et de renom;
> Pour deux grandes princesses
> Je perds ma royauté:
> L'une a fait le plus grand des rois;
> L'autre le tient dessous ses lois;
> Pour vous, grandes princesses,
> Je perds ma royauté.

This complimentary address was most graciously received by both queens, and obtained a flattering response from Marie de Médicis.

Venus then presented a golden apple to Henriette Marie, and Pallas laid her spear and shield at the princess's feet. This done, the Olympian troop retired, and shortly afterwards the three royal ladies arose and retired to an ante-chamber.

Presently, the orchestra again struck up, and the ball commenced with a coranto, in which a vast number of couples took part. Then followed a bransle, and while this was going on, the Duc de Montbazon made his way to Charles and his companions, and besought them to follow him.

As soon as they were out of the crowd, Montbazon said to the prince, "The queen is about to dance a saraband with the Princess Henriette Marie, the Comtesse de la Torre, and the Comtesse Monteleone, and it is her majesty's desire that your highness and my lord of Buckingham take part in the dance."

"I am fully sensible of the honour intended me, M. le Duc," replied Charles, "but I must pray you to make my excuses to the queen."

"I dare not deliver such an answer, prince," rejoined Montbazon. "Her majesty is not accustomed to refusal. I must entreat you to make your excuses in person. Do you, my lord," he added to Buckingham, "decline the proffered honour?"

"Decline it! Heaven forbid!" exclaimed Buckingham. "I am entirely at her majesty's disposal —in this as in all other matters."

Montbazon then conducted Charles and his companions to the ante-room, whither the two queens had retired. Here they found Marie de Médicis, with four ladies attired in magnificent Spanish dresses, each of different coloured silk, but all richly embroidered with fringes of gold, and ornamented with knots of ribands. Though these ladies were masked, it was not difficult to distinguish in two of them the queen and the princess.

Anne of Austria wore a yellow satin basquina, which suited her exquisite figure to perfection, and Henriette Marie was attired in a blush-coloured dress of the same material and make, which became her equally well. The Comtesse de Torre and the Comtesse Monteleone were dressed respectively in white and blue.

On entering the room, Montbazon advanced to the queen and said a few words to her, on hearing which she manifested her disappointment by a slight impatient gesture, but desired him to bring forward the prince and his companions.

This was done, and they were presented, but under what designations Charles did not hear.

" The Duc de Montbazon tells me, prince," said Anne of Austria, in a slight tone of pique, " that you are unwilling to dance with me."

" Not unwilling, madame," replied Charles, " but unable. I do not dance the saraband."

"It is the easiest dance imaginable," said the queen. " I wish you would try it."

"I dare not, madame," returned Charles. "I should only be an embarrassment to your majesty, and incur the ridicule of the company."

" Have courage and make the attempt, prince," cried Henriette Marie. "We will take care you shall make no mistake."

" Even with this encouragement I will not venture," returned Charles. "I shall not rise in your opinion if I confess that I care little for lively figures, and confine myself to the pavane and pazzameno."

"The pavane is my favourite dance," cried the princess.

"Were it given, I would ask to be your partner," said Charles, gallantly.

"The princess will be charmed to dance with you," said Marie de Médicis, answering for her daughter. "After the saraband we will have a pavane."

"The Duc de Montbazon tells me you are going to Spain, prince," said Anne of Austria to Charles. "You ought, therefore, to learn our national dances."

"I will practise them at Madrid," returned the prince. "But though I am unskilled in the saraband, the Marquis of Buckingham is not. May I offer him as my substitute in the dance?"

"I have heard that my Lord of Buckingham is the most graceful dancer in Europe," remarked the queen. "I am curious to know whether the report is correct."

"I am sorry your majesty's expectations have

been so highly raised, as I shall probably disappoint them," rejoined Buckingham.

" I have a passion for dancing—and of all dances those of Spain delight me most. But I have never yet found a partner who could dance the saraband with me."

"Perhaps you will make the same complaint of me to-morrow," returned the queen.

" Impossible, madame," said Buckingham. " There is much more likelihood that I shall sink in your opinion."

"At all events, I promise to be lenient to your faults," rejoined Anne of Austria, smiling.

At this moment two young Spanish noblemen entered the room, and, on beholding them, the queen exclaimed that the party was complete, and calling for castanets, which were handed to all those about to dance the saraband, bade the Duc de Montbazon order the band to strike up. The order was promptly obeyed, and while inspiriting strains animated the whole assemblage, the four couples issued from the ante-room into the grand saloon. Graham had the distinguished honour of leading out the Princess Henriette Marie. All were masked, but as it was generally known that the queen and the princess were the chief dancers, great curiosity was excited.

In another moment the dancers had taken up their position, and as they threw themselves into a graceful preliminary attitude, every eye was fixed upon them. Nothing could be more exquisite than the posture assumed by the queen; it was beautiful, disdainful, and full of witchery. In another moment the merry rattle of castanets was heard, and the dance began.

Every movement of Anne of Austria was marked by the same grace that distinguished her in repose, and each turn of the dance served to reveal fresh beauties. Alternately she appeared to be excited by coquetry, agitated by gentle emotions of love, stirred by jealousy, and inflamed by rage. All these emotions were admirably portrayed, while the most difficult steps were executed with consummate ease and grace, and with inconceivable rapidity.

Buckingham well sustained his character as the best dancer of his day. So much grace and agility had never before been displayed in that hall by any devotee of Terpsichore.

If the Princess Henriette Marie did not display the fire and passion exhibited by the queen, or possess in so high a degree as her majesty the poetry of motion, she acquitted herself charmingly, and delighted Charles, who watched her movements with admiration.

While the saraband was proceeding, the king entered the saloon, and his attention being drawn to Buckingham, he inquired who he was, and not being able to obtain the information from those around him, sent for the Duc de Montbazon.

"Who is the queen's partner?" demanded Louis, as the duke came up.

"An English nobleman, sire," replied Montbazon, without hesitation.

"An English nobleman!" exclaimed the king, surprised. "I concluded he was a Spaniard. He dances like a hidalgo. His name—and title?"

"I find it impossible to pronounce his name, sire, so you must excuse my attempting it, but he is a person of high rank."

"You are quite sure he is an Englishman, M. le Duc? He has not the air of one."

"I am quite sure of it, sire. There are two other Englishmen of rank in the ball-room—one of whom is dancing with the Princess Henriette Marie. They are merely passing through Paris on their way to Madrid, so I have not presented them to your majesty."

"Did I not deem it impossible, I should say that the person dancing with the queen must be the Marquis of Buckingham," observed the Comte d'Auvergne.

"Perhaps it is Buckingham," cried the Duc de Luynes.

"Bah!" exclaimed Louis. "The notion is absurd. You might as well assert the Prince of Wales is in the room."

"Just as well, sire,—one assertion is as likely as the other," said Montbazon. And anxious to avoid further explanation, he craved leave to withdraw.

By this time the saraband had concluded, and the dancers returned to the ante-room.

Anne of Austria seated herself on a fauteuil, but did not dismiss Buckingham, who remained standing near her. Charles also had re-entered the room and approached the Princess Henriette Marie, who had taken a seat beside the queen-mother.

"You must be too much fatigued with your exertions to go through the pavane, princess," he observed.

"Dancing never fatigues me," she replied. "It is the pleasantest exercise one can take. I prefer it to hawking and hunting."

"I have ever preferred the tilt-yard to the ball-room," returned Charles; "but were I to remain long at this court my tastes would certainly undergo a change."

"You flatter me by saying so, prince. But I do not entirely believe you."

"Nay, it is truth," said Charles, gallantly.

"Here comes the Duc de Montbazon to announce that the pavane is about to begin," observed Marie de Médicis to her daughter. "Are you ready?"

"Quite," replied Henriette Marie. "I need no further repose."

And rising at the same time, she gave her hand to Charles, who led her into the saloon.

The appearance of the princess served as a signal to the orchestra, and the other couples being already placed, the dance at once commenced.

The stately character of the pavane, all the movements of which were slow and dignified, displayed Charles's majestic deportment to the utmost advantage, and he excited quite as much admiration as Buckingham had just done in the sparkling saraband.

That two such stars, each so brilliant, though differing in splendour, should appear at the same time, was sufficient to cause excitement, and general inquiries began to be made as to who the distinguished strangers could be. But though many conjectures were hazarded, all were wide of the mark.

In Henriette Marie the prince found a partner every way worthy of him. If she did not rival him in dignity, she equalled him in grace, and Charles himself, who had been struck by the vivacity exhibited by the princess in the previous dance, was surprised by the stateliness she now displayed.

XIII.

HOW TOM FELL DESPERATELY IN LOVE.

MEANTIME, Buckingham remained in the ante-room, standing beside Anne of Austria, whose charms had already inspired him with a passion so violent, that he would have sacrificed the expedition on which he was bent, and the prince whom he attended, to obtain one favouring smile from her. Such was his overweening vanity, such the confidence he felt in his own irresistible powers of fascination, that he persuaded himself that the queen was not insensible to his admiration.

Careless of any consequences that might ensue

should he be recognised, he had removed his mask. His looks breathed passion, and to every light word he uttered he sought to convey tender significance. Whether from coquetry, or that Buckingham's admiration was not disagreeable to her, certain it is that the queen did not reprove his audacity; and thus emboldened, he well-nigh forgot that many curious eyes were watching him, many ears listening to catch his words.

"And so you depart to-morrow for Madrid, my lord?" said the queen.

"The prince has so arranged it, madame," returned Buckingham, "but at a word from you, I stay."

"Nay, I cannot detain you," she rejoined. "Would I were going thither myself!" she added, with a sigh. "But I shall never more behold the city I love so well — never more set foot in the palace where the happiest hours of my life were spent."

"You surprise me, madame," cried Buckingham. "Is it possible that, occupying your present splendid position as sovereign mistress of this brilliant court, you can have any regrets for the past?"

"Splendour of position is not everything, my lord," returned Anne of Austria. "I was happier as the Infanta than I am as Queen of France." Then feeling she had said too much, she added, "To you, my lord, I will venture to utter what I would confide to few others. My heart is in Spain —I am still a stranger here, and shall ever continue so. When you see my sister, the Infanta Maria, repeat my words to her."

"I will do whatever your majesty enjoins, though your regrets for Spain may make the Infanta loth to quit her native land."

"Ah! but your prince will reconcile her to the step—I am sure of it. I can read loyalty and devotion in his noble features. Where Charles Stuart gives his hand he will give his whole heart."

" You are an excellent physiognomist, madame," said Buckingham. " You have read the prince's character aright."

" Then my sister will be truly fortunate if she wins him. You say I am a good physiognomist, my lord, but your opinion will alter, I fear, when I declare that I see inconstancy written in your features as plainly as fidelity is stamped on those of the Prince of Wales."

" There your majesty is undoubtedly in error," returned Buckingham. " What you say may be true of the past, because till now my heart has never been touched. But the impression it has this night received is indelible as it is vivid."

And he threw a passionate glance at the queen, who cast down her eyes.

" Has not your majesty some slight token of regard that I may convey to the Infanta ?" he inquired. " It would make me more welcome to her."

" I have nothing to send," replied the queen.

"Had I known you were going to Madrid beforehand, I might have been prepared. Stay, take this," she added, giving him a small, richly-chased vinaigrette, at which she had just breathed.

Buckingham took it rapturously.

"My sister will recollect it, and will know it comes from me," said Anne of Austria.

"I may not keep it, then?" rejoined Buckingham, imploringly. "'Twill be hard to part with it."

"I do not insist upon your delivering it," returned the queen. "But such a trifle is not worth keeping."

Buckingham's looks showed that he thought far otherwise.

Here it was well that this brief but dangerous interview was terminated by the return of Charles and Henriette Marie.

It was not without a severe pang that Buckingham tore himself away from one who had gained such a sudden and complete ascendancy over him.

Fickle he had ever hitherto been in affairs of the heart, but he now submitted to the force of a great and overpowering passion. Nor could he liberate himself from it. Anne of Austria ever afterwards remained sovereign mistress of his heart, and his insane passion for her led him to commit acts of inconceivable folly.

Charles, as we have said, had returned with his fair partner to the ante-chamber, and on seeing them the queen signed to Henriette Marie to take a seat beside her. The princess obeyed, and as she sat down it was easy to perceive from her looks that she had enjoyed the dance, and Anne was making a remark to that effect, when the Duc de Montbazon came suddenly into the room, and made his way without ceremony to Charles, who was standing with Buckingham near the queen.

"What is the matter, M. le Duc?" cried Anne of Austria, seeing, from his manner, that something was wrong.

"The prince and his attendants must quit the

Louvre immediately," returned Montbazon. "The king has been struck by their appearance, and has been making inquiries about them, but has failed in obtaining any precise information. Unluckily, my son, the Comte de Rochefort, who has been in England, has made a guess not far wide of the truth, and his majesty's suspicions having become aroused, he will not rest till they are satisfied. Under these circumstances," he added, turning to Charles, "your highness's wisest course will be to depart at once."

"Where is the king?" demanded Anne of Austria, uneasily.

"Madame, he is in the ball-room at this moment," replied Montbazon; "but he is certain to come hither before long, and if he finds the prince and my Lord of Buckingham with your majesty, it will be impossible to prevent a discovery; and then I much fear the meditated journey to Madrid will have to be postponed."

"That must not be," cried the queen. "Fly,

prince," she added to Charles. "Stand upon no ceremony, but begone. Adieu, my lord," she said to Buckingham; "forget not my message to my sister."

And as he bent before her she extended her hand to him, and he fervently pressed it to his lips.

"Adieu, princess," said Charles to Henriette Marie; "I had hoped to dance the pazzameno with you, but that is now impossible."

"So it seems," replied Henriette Marie. "I am almost selfish enough to desire you might be detained. But since you must go, I wish you a safe and pleasant journey to Madrid. Adieu, prince."

Charles then made a profound obeisance to Marie de Médicis, as did Buckingham and Graham, the latter having emerged from an embrasure, where he had been chatting with the Comtesse de la Torre. All three then quitted the room, and one of them, as we are aware, left his heart behind him. By the advice of the Duc de Montbazon, they kept on the right of the grand saloon, and so avoided the king, who was on the other side of the hall.

Ever self-possessed, Charles manifested no undue haste, but moved majestically through the long suite of apartments which he had previously traversed.

Among the pages and attendants collected in the grand corridor was Chevilly, and on seeing the prince and his companions, and finding they desired to depart, he conducted them to the vestibule, where he left them while he summoned their carriage.

In a few minutes he reappeared, ushered them to the coach, and, posted on the marche-pied as before, attended them to their hotel. On dismissing him, the prince rewarded him with a dozen pistoles.

It was fortunate for the success of Charles's project that he did not delay his departure. He had not quitted the ante-room many minutes when the king entered it. His majesty's countenance appeared disturbed, and he glanced inquisitively round the room.

"Where are those Englishmen?" he said abruptly to the queen. "I was told they were here."

"They are gone, sire," replied Anne. "I am sorry for it. They dance remarkably well. Don't you think so, sire?"

"I scarcely noticed their dancing," rejoined Louis, sharply. "But I want to know who they are."

"You must apply to the Duc de Montbazon then, sire," said the queen. "They are English noblemen, that is all I can tell you."

"Their rank is undoubted, sire," remarked Marie de Médicis. "You may take my assurance for that."

"You know them, madame?" cried Louis.

"I do," she replied. "But I am not at liberty to disclose their names to-night. To-morrow I will tell you who they are. Suspend your curiosity till then."

With this the king was obliged to be content, and soon afterwards returned to the ball-room, but in no very good humour.

Before retiring to rest, Charles wrote a long letter to his august father, describing his journey to Paris, and detailing all that had befallen him since his arrival in the French capital. Besides recording his impressions of the principal personages he had seen at the Luxembourg and the Louvre, Charles spoke in rapturous terms of the beauty of Anne of Austria, but he did not praise the Princess Henriette Marie as highly as she deserved. To have said all he thought of her, might have appeared like disloyalty to the Infanta. Buckingham at the same time indited a humorous epistle to his dear dad and gossip.

As soon as these despatches were completed, they were consigned to a courier who was waiting for them, and who started, without a moment's delay, for Calais.

"Henriette Marie is very charming," thought

Charles, as he sought his couch. "I cannot get her out of my head."

"Anne of Austria is the loveliest creature on earth," cried Buckingham, as he paced to and fro within his chamber, thinking over the events of the evening. "I am in despair at quitting Paris. Yet I must go."

XIV.

IN WHAT MANNER JACK AND TOM LEFT PARIS, AND OF THE ADVENTURE THEY MET WITH IN THE FOREST OF ORLÉANS.

NEXT morning, at a very early hour, Charles was aroused from his slumbers by Cottington, who entered the prince's chamber with a light.

"Is it time to arise, Cottington?" demanded Charles, drowsily.

"Your highness can rest as long as you please," replied the other. "Since midnight, an order has been sent by the king to all postmasters, prohibiting them to supply us with horses. It will be impossible, therefore, for your highness to leave Paris."

"But I will not be stayed!" cried Charles, starting up in his couch. "I will buy horses if I cannot hire them. See to it, Cottington—see to it."

"Permit me to observe to your highness that horses are not to be bought at this untimely hour, and, before we can procure them, in all probability a further order will be issued by the king interdicting your departure from Paris."

"Call my lord of Buckingham, and bid him come to me instantly," cried Charles.

But before the order could be obeyed, Graham burst into the chamber, exclaiming: "Good news! good news! your highness will be able to start for Madrid after all. M. Chevilly is without, and says he can remove the new difficulty that has arisen."

"That is good news indeed, Dick!" cried Charles. "Let him come in. Good-morrow, Chevilly," he added, as the valet made his appearance. "What can you do for us?"

"I can help your highness to leave Paris," replied Chevilly. "The duke my master has sent you horses. They are the best in his stables, and will carry you twenty or thirty leagues with ease. A piqueur and two palefreniers will go with you to bring them back. If I may presume to do so, I would respectfully counsel your highness to start as speedily as may be, for fear of further interruption."

"Your counsel is good, Chevilly, and shall not be neglected," returned Charles. "Let all prepare for immediate departure."

On this the chamber was cleared, and Charles, springing from his couch, proceeded to attire himself for the journey.

Meantime, under the careful surveillance of Chevilly, the superb steeds, sent for the use of the prince and his attendants by the considerate Duc de Montbazon, were saddled and bridled by the palefreniers, who next proceeded to secure the pack-saddles, containing the baggage, on their own hackneys.

In less than half an hour all necessary preparations were completed, and shortly afterwards Charles and Buckingham, accoutred in their new riding-dresses, boots, and broad-leaved hats, entered the salle à manger, where the rest of the party were assembled. Such was the prince's impatience to be gone, that he declined to partake of the breakfast that had been prepared for him, and thrusting a pair of pistols into his belt, and throwing a cartouche-belt over his shoulder, called out, " To horse, gentlemen, to horse!"

Marshalled by the host, whose account had already been discharged by Endymion Porter, the whole party repaired to the court-yard, where the steeds were impatiently pawing the ground. Charles selected a powerful black charger for his own use, and Buckingham made choice of a magnificent grey.

"I trust the duke your master will not incur his majesty's displeasure by the service he has rendered me," said Charles to Chevilly, as the latter held his stirrup.

"My master promised the queen that your highness's departure should not be prevented—and he has kept his word," replied the valet.

"Fail not to make my best acknowledgments to him," said Charles, bestowing a handful of pistoles on Chevilly as he vaulted into the saddle. "Farewell, friend."

In another minute, the whole party being mounted, the gates of the hotel were thrown open, and the cavalcade issued forth into the Rue dé Bourbon, preceded by the piqueur.

But for this avant garde, who answered all questions satisfactorily, they must have been stopped by the watch. Having traversed the Rue Jacob, the Rue Colombier, and several other sombre streets, they skirted the high walls surrounding the close of the great convent of Carthusians, and at last reached the Barrière d'Enfer, where they were detained for a short time, as the gate was not yet opened, and the warder refused to let them pass, but on the production by the piqueur of an order from the Duc de Montbazon, the obstacle was removed, and they were allowed to proceed on their journey.

No sooner were they clear of the Faubourg Saint Jacques, than, setting spurs to their steeds, they galloped along the high road to Orléans, passing without halt, or slackening of pace, through Bourg la Reine, Sceaux, and Berny, and never pausing till they reached Longjumeau, where they pulled up for a few minutes at a cabaret to refresh their horses and drink a cup of wine.

The arrival of the cavalcade in the little town at this early hour in the morning—it was then only seven o'clock—created quite a sensation, and many of the inhabitants flocked towards the cabaret to look at them. All knew, from their horses and attendants, that they must be persons of rank, but the piqueur, though questioned by the aubergiste and the garçons d'écurie, would give no information, except that they were English noblemen.

Neither Charles nor Buckingham dismounted, and their distinguished appearance pointed them out as the chief personages of the troop. After they had drunk a flagon of Anjou wine, which was handed them by the hôtelier, Charles exclaimed,

"What ails you, Tom? You have not uttered a word since we left Paris. I never knew you so silent before."

"I have been thinking of that divine queen," responded Buckingham. "But you have been equally silent, Jack. I suspect, from your pensive air, that your thoughts have been occupied by the charming princess. Am I not right?"

"Her image will recur to me, I own," rejoined Charles. "But henceforward I shall banish it, and think only of the Infanta. But we have stayed

here long enough. Allons, messieurs!" he cried
to his attendants.

At the words, Cottington and the two others,
who were standing at the door of the cabaret
talking to the host, instantly mounted their steeds,
the palefreniers followed their example, and the
piqueur, taking off his cap to Charles, rode on
in advance. The whole party then set off at a
gallop, and were soon out of sight.

On, on they went, flying like the wind past the
old château of Mont-Lhéry, perched on its rocky
heights, and traversing a pleasant country, erst
dyed with Burgundian blood, clearing league after
league without fatigue to themselves, and apparently without fatigue to their gallant coursers,
until they reached Arpajan.

After a brief halt they again set forward, speeding on swiftly as before, devouring the distance
that lay between the pretty little town they had
just quitted and Etrecy.

By this time both Charles and Buckingham,

having quite recovered their spirits, laughed and chatted merrily. Everything contributed to make their journey agreeable—a fine day, and a charming country, presenting a succession of lovely landscapes.

How rapidly and easily we get on," cried Charles. "These admirable horses will spoil us for the rest of the journey. It is a pity we shall lose them at Etampes."

"I see no reason for that," rejoined Buckingham. "With an hour's rest they will carry us several leagues farther. If they should be harmed, which is not likely, we will replace them by horses from England."

On arriving at Etampes, Charles consulted the piqueur, who said:

"Monseigneur, with an hour's rest here, and another hour at Artenay, the horses will carry you very well to Orléans."

"But that is more than the duke your master bargained for, my good friend," said Charles.

"Pardon, monseigneur. My master has placed the horses entirely at your disposal," rejoined the piqueur. "Do as you please with them."

"Then you shall go on with us to Orléans," said Charles. "We will not part with the horses a league sooner than necessary."

After the lapse of an hour, during which the horses had been well cared for, and their riders recruited by a plentiful repast and several flasks of excellent wine, the whole party got once more into the saddle, and were soon scouring across the broad and fertile plains of La Beauce, in the direction of Montdésir. Acting on the piqueur's suggestions, Charles and his companions made another halt at Artenay, and then set forward again.

Night was now rapidly approaching, and it soon became quite dark. Moreover, just as they entered the Forest of Orléans—a vast woody region of some leagues in extent, which lay between them and that city—a heavy thunderstorm came on, accompanied by torrents of rain. No place of shelter being near, there was nothing for it but to brave the storm, so, wrapping their cloaks around them, they went on. Peal after peal of thunder rattled overhead, and the flashes of lightning were almost blinding. Still the piqueur rode gallantly on, and the cavalcade followed him.

Despite the personal inconvenience he endured, the storm excited Charles's admiration. One moment all was buried in obscurity; the next, the whole thicket seemed in a blaze. Thus shown by the vivid flashes, the trees looked so weird and fantastic, that it almost seemed to the prince as if he was riding through an enchanted forest. For some time the cavalcade, headed by the piqueur, went on without interruption, but at last the broken state of the ground compelled them to proceed with caution.

Suddenly the piqueur came to a stop, and owned that he had missed his way. But he felt certain, he said, that he could soon regain it. A consultation was then held as to the best course to be pursued under the circumstances. Buckingham and some of the others were for turning back, but Charles, believing the piqueur could get them out of the difficulty, determined to go on.

Accordingly, the cavalcade got once more into motion, but now proceeded at a foot's pace. The alley which they were threading was of considerable length, but it brought them in the end to an open space, in the midst of which grew three or four trees of the largest size and great age, veritable patriarchs of the grove. But here the difficulties of the travellers appeared to have increased, for though there were several outlets from the clearance they had gained, they could not tell which to select.

While they were in this state of incertitude, it was with no slight satisfaction that they descried through the gloom a figure approaching them. As this person drew nearer, the lightning showed him to be a powerfully-built man, in the garb of a peasant. Probably a woodcutter, as he carried a hatchet on his shoulder.

"What ho, master!" cried the piqueur, calling out to him. "Wilt guide us to the high road to Orléans?"

"Ay, marry will I," replied the woodcutter; "but you have strayed far away from it, and are not likely to find it again without help. It is lucky for you that I came up, or you might have passed the night in the forest."

"Is there no place where we can dry our wet apparel and obtain refreshment?" said Charles.

"You cannot do better than come to my cottage, messieurs," replied the man. "My name is Jacques Leroux. I am a woodcutter, as my father was before me, and my grandfather before him, and as my sons André and Marcel will be after me; but I have saved some money, and live comfortably enough, as you will see. Many a traveller who has missed his way in the forest, as you have

done to-night, has fared well—though I say it—
and slept soundly at my cottage."

"Perchance too soundly," remarked Buckingham, with a laugh. "Well, we will go to thy
cottage, honest Jacques," he continued, "and
when the storm is over thou shalt take us to the
road to Orléans, and we will reward thee handsomely."

"The storm will be over in an hour," said
Jacques Leroux, "and then the moon will have
risen. Once on the highway, you will soon reach
Orléans."

"I am glad to hear it," cried Buckingham.
"Canst give us aught for supper, honest Jacques?"

"My larder is not badly supplied," replied the
woodcutter, with a laugh, "and I have a few
flasks of rare Beaugency in my cellar."

"Nay, if thou hast a larder and cellar we shall
not fare badly," said Buckingham. "Lead us to
thy cottage, good Jacques."

"This way, messieurs," returned the wood-cutter, striking into an alley on the right, which proved so narrow and intricate that the horsemen were obliged to proceed along it singly. Jacques Leroux, however, being familiar with the path, tracked it without difficulty, and at a quick pace, but he ever and anon stopped to cheer on those behind him.

"You appear to be taking us into the heart of the forest, friend," cried Charles, who was at the head of the column.

"You are within a bow-shot of my dwelling, monsieur," replied the woodcutter. "You will see the lights in a moment. I will let my daughter know I am coming," he added, placing a whistle to his lips, and blowing a shrill and somewhat startling call.

Immediately afterwards the troop emerged upon a patch of ground entirely free from timber. In the midst of this area stood a cottage, with a stable and some other outbuildings attached to it.

Again Jacques Leroux blew his whistle, and no sooner had he done so than the cottage door was thrown open, allowing the radiance of a cheerful fire to stream forth. Just within the threshold might be seen a young woman, and a boy some ten or twelve years old, whom the woodcutter informed Charles were his youngest son Marcel, and his daughter Rose.

"Our young foresters call her Rose des Bois," said Jacques, with a laugh, "and several of them are anxious to take her from me, but I don't desire to part with her just yet. Will it please you to alight, messieurs? You need have no anxiety about the horses. There is a stable large enough to hold them all, and Marcel will find them plenty of good fodder."

"You seem well provided with everything, friend," observed Charles, as he alighted.

"Heaven be praised, I want nothing, and am well contented with my lot," replied the woodcutter.

By this time the whole party had alighted, and Jacques called to his son to bring a lantern and help the palefreniers to take the horses to the stable. This order being promptly obeyed, the woodcutter ushered his guests into his dwelling, and on passing through the doorway Charles and his companions found themselves in a large comfortable room, cheerfully illumined by a wood fire, which was blazing on the hearthstone.

Benches were set on either side of the wide-mouthed chimney, and in the middle of the room there was a large oak table, with several stools placed around it. A gammon of bacon, a goodly stock of hams, with other dried meats depending from the rafters, showed that the cottage did not lack the materials of good cheer, while an open cupboard displayed a large pasty, a cheese, eggs, butter, and an abundant supply of bread—far more than seemed to be required by the woodcutter and his family.

Besides these unmistakable evidences of plenty,

which were very satisfactory to the travellers, a large black iron pot, hanging from a hook over the fire, diffused an odour throughout the chamber that left no doubt as to the savoury nature of its contents.

At the moment the party entered, the wood-cutter's daughter was placing fresh logs on the fire, and as she turned to salute them, they were all struck by her good looks, and Charles remarked to her father that she well deserved her appellation of Rose des Bois.

The damsel, who might be about eighteen, had a rich dark complexion, bright black eyes, somewhat too bold, perhaps, in expression, hair black as jet, and growing low down on the forehead, and strongly marked, handsome eyebrows. She wore large gold earrings, gold ornaments in her lace cap, and a gold cross above her bodice. The skirts of her scarlet petticoat were short enough to display her well-formed limbs, and her sabots were no disfigurement to her trim ankles and small feet. The drawbacks to her beauty were the bold looks we have mentioned, and a somewhat masculine manner.

She eyed the travellers with unrestrained curiosity, and though she could rarely have seen such visitors, did not appear at all abashed. Graham, however, chiefly attracted her attention, and she more than once regarded him fixedly.

Throwing off their cloaks, the travellers seated themselves on the benches near the fire, to dry their wet apparel. While they were thus disposed, and active preparations for supper were being made by Jacques and his daughter, the latter of whom was spreading a snow-white cloth on the table, the two palefreniers entered with the saddle-bags which Endymion Porter had ordered to be brought into the cottage. On perceiving this arrangement, which he had evidently not anticipated, a cloud came over the woodcutter's brow, and he cast a significant look at his daughter.

The look did not escape Graham, and from its

peculiarity awakened his suspicions. He said nothing, however, but, getting up from the bench, sat down near the table, and while chatting gaily with Rose, kept a watchful eye upon her father.

Having placed a large pasty, with other cold provisions, on the table, Jacques Leroux told his daughter that he was going to fetch a few flasks of Beaugency, and quitted the chamber by a side-door. No sooner was he gone than Rose drew close to Graham, and said, in a low tone,

"What has brought you here?"

"We came by your father's invitation," replied the young man, in the same tone.

"Jacques Leroux is not my father," replied Rose. "But no matter. What it concerns you to know is, that you are in danger of your life. You may have heard that the Forest of Orléans is infested by a band of robbers. Jacques Leroux is their captain. He has contrived to ensnare you, and, be assured, he will not let you escape."

"Bah! we are too numerous a party, and too

well armed, to fear attack," rejoined Graham. "You want to frighten me away, my pretty Rose. But I will not go, unless you will consent to accompany me."

"You think I am jesting, but I am in earnest, as you will find. You heard Jacques whistle as he approached the cottage. That was a signal to a scout, who immediately started to collect the band. They will be here presently."

"'Sdeath! this is more serious than I thought," said Graham, uneasily. "I must alarm my friends."

"On no account," she replied, imposing silence upon him by a look.

At this moment Jacques Leroux entered, carrying half a dozen flasks of wine, three of which he set upon the table, but he put the others aside.

"Don't drink that wine—it is drugged," whispered Rose des Bois.

"I am half inclined to blow out the rascal's

brains," said Graham, laying his hand upon a pistol.

Just then the outer door of the cottage was opened, and a young man, in a woodcutter's garb like that of Leroux, came in, and respectfully saluted the strangers.

"So you are returned from Courcelles, André," remarked Jacques, with a significant look at him. "Have you executed all my orders?"

"All, father," replied André.

"The band have arrived," whispered Rose des Bois. "But trust to me, and I will save you."

"By my faith, this is a devoted damsel," thought Graham. "But though I am willing to trust her, on the first movement made by these villains that looks like mischief I will shoot them, be the consequences what they may. The prince has been dying for an adventure—he has met with one at last. Hark'ee, my pretty Rose des Bois," he added, in an under tone to her. "There are far more valuable lives than mine at stake. None of my companions must be harmed."

"Trust to me, and you shall all get away safely," she replied.

As she spoke, the sound of horses was heard outside, and André, opening the door, exclaimed,

"There are more travellers here, father. What shall we do with their horses ? The stable is full."

"Put them in the shed," replied Jacques. And he went out with his son, closing the door after him.

Scarcely were they gone, than Rose hastily removed the flasks which Jacques had set upon the table, and put the three others in their place.

"You may drink this wine with safety," she said to Graham.

Shortly afterwards, Jacques and André returned with half a dozen persons of very suspicious mien. As the new comers took off their cloaks and broad-leaved hats, it appeared they were all well armed with pistols and swords.

On their appearance, Charles and his companions moved from the fireside to the table.

"I have so many guests here to-night, messieurs," said Jacques to the new comers, "that I shall not be able to offer you very good accommodation. But I will do my best."

"That is all we require," said the foremost of the party. "You can give us a flask of good wine—that we know from experience."

"Ay, that I can—as good as you will get at Orléans," rejoined Jacques. "Pray be seated near the fire," he added, pointing to the benches vacated by Charles and his companions. "I will bring you the wine immediately, but I must first serve these gentlemen, who are waiting for supper."

With this, he proceeded to uncork the flasks which had just been set on the table by Rose, and filled the goblets for Charles and his companions.

"This is the Beaugency I spoke of, messieurs," he said. "It has a rare flavour. I will venture to say you never tasted wine equal to it."

"Then I propose a bumper all round," cried Graham, glancing at his companions. "Fill for yonder gentlemen, Maître Jacques."

"Ay, fill us bumpers, Jacques," shouted the guests at the fireplace.

"This flask is empty. I will bring you another, messieurs," cried the woodcutter, taking up one of those which Rose had removed.

While he was occupied in filling the flagons of the party near the fire, Rose whispered a word or two in Graham's ear.

"Nay, you and your son must join us, my good friend," cried the latter to Jacques.

"Doubt me not," replied the woodcutter, laughing. "Bring two more flagons, André."

The young man brought him the cups, which he instantly filled.

"To your health, messieurs!" cried Graham. "If you are the boon companions you seem, you will not leave a drop in the cup."

With this he emptied his goblet, and turned it

upside down. All those at the table did the same.

"They are ours now," remarked Jacques, winking at his associates.

"You seem to hesitate, messieurs," cried Graham. "We have set you a good example."

"Hesitate—not we!" responded the foremost of the brigands. "To your healths, messieurs! May you always meet with honest men like us!"

And the whole party emptied their flagons, their example being followed by Jacques and André.

"By my faith, friend Jacques, this Beaugency of yours is a most powerful wine," cried Graham. "It has already got into my head. I feel quite drowsy."

"So do we," cried the others at the table.

"Take another cup—it won't hurt you," responded Jacques.

"Fill for me, then," said Graham.

As the woodcutter approached the table, he staggered and fell to the ground. André sprang to his father's assistance, but while trying to raise him, he also sank on the floor in a state of stupefaction.

"What's the matter?" cried Graham, rising from his chair. "Have you and your son been taken suddenly ill, my good friend?"

"We have drunk the wrong wine," cried Jacques to his comrades, trying in vain to rise.

"Malediction!" exclaimed the foremost of the brigands, tumbling from the bench.

So powerless had he and his comrades become, that not one of them could draw a pistol. In vain they struggled against the effects of the soporific potion they had swallowed. In another minute they were all buried in a profound stupor.

"We have had a narrow escape," cried Graham. "We owe our lives, perhaps, to this damsel."

"Let us quit the place immediately, and make the best of our way to Orléans," said Charles.

"You must take me with you," said Rose des

Bois. " If I am left here, when these men recover they will infallibly put me to death."

" Do not imagine we are going to abandon you, after what you have done for us," replied Graham. " We will take you with us to Orléans, and, moreover, you shall be well rewarded."

Leaving the senseless brigands, the party then went forth, and, guided by Rose, proceeded towards the stable. Close to the building they found Marcel, who tried to escape on seeing them, but, being caught by Graham, the lad gave up the key of the stable, in which he had contrived to lock up the piqueur and palefreniers, who were clamouring lustily to get out. Without loss of time the men were set free, and the horses brought out. The pack-saddles were then fetched from the cottage, and being secured as before, the whole party mounted their steeds. As Jacques Leroux had predicted, the storm had passed away. Still, though the moon was now shining brightly, and tipping the trees with silver, it was necessary to have a guide through the forest, so the travellers determined to take Marcel with them, and accordingly placed him in front of the piqueur, who had orders to shoot him if he misled them. The next point was how to convey Rose des Bois. This was settled by Graham, who took her on his saddle-bow.

All these arrangements being made with great expedition, the party set off, and following Marcel's directions, eventually reached the high road to Orléans.

Before this, however, the lad had contrived to loosen the belt by which he was bound to the piqueur, and, watching his opportunity, slipped off the horse; and, though the piqueur fired at him, he escaped uninjured, and disappeared among the trees. His flight, however, gave the party no concern.

In half an hour more they had cleared the forest, and had gained the faubourg of the ancient city of Orléans.

On reaching these habitations, Rose des Bois said to Graham:

"Here we must part. But whither are you going?"

"I am going far hence, my pretty Rose," he replied.

"But where?" she demanded, impatiently. "Tell me where."

"To Madrid," he replied. "It is not likely we shall meet again."

"Perhaps we may. Farewell!"

And, disengaging herself, she sprang lightly to the ground.

Graham offered her his purse, but she refused it with an impatient gesture, and hurried away.

The party then rode on to the gates of Orléans, and not without some difficulty obtained admittance to the city. This being at last accomplished, they proceeded to the Hôtel du Loiret, and entered it just as the bell of the cathedral tolled the hour of midnight.

XV.

HOW JACK AND TOM RODE TO BORDEAUX, AND HOW THEY
RECEIVED A VISIT FROM THE DUC D'EPERNON.

NEXT morning, at seven o'clock, our travellers
started once more on their journey, mounted on
post-horses, and attended by a couple of postilions.

Before setting out, Charles liberally rewarded
the piqueur and the palefreniers, who undertook
that the ends of justice should not be neglected,
and promised to obtain from the magistrates of
the city a force sufficient for the capture of the
brigands. This, we may state, was effected the

same day, and the whole band brought prisoners to Orléans.

Our impatient travellers saw nothing of the ancient city, which derives its chief interest from the heroic and ill-fated Jeanne d'Arc, save what was presented to them as. they traversed the streets to the Porte de Blois.

Their road now lay on the right bank of the Loire, and throughout the day they kept near that enchanting river, which mirrors on its waves such lovely vine-clad slopes and hills, and such picturesque old towns and grand feudal châteaux. Blois and Amboise, with their regal castles, detained the travellers for a short time, and it was not until nightfall that they reached Tours.

Off again next morning betimes, they approached Châtelleraut about noon, and traversing the antique bridge across the Vienne, garnished at either end with towers, they entered the town, and resting there for an hour, pursued their way to Poitiers, where they arrived sufficiently early to devote some time to the examination of a town replete with historical recollections, many of them of deep interest to Charles.

Before retiring to rest they heard vespers in the cathedral, and after attending matins in the beautiful church of Sainte Radegonde, and visiting several other interesting structures, they started for Angoulême, arriving there, after a brief halt at Civray, early in the evening.

Again early in the saddle, and descending the steep hill on which Angoulême is reared, they speeded merrily along the valley, the limit of their day's journey being Bordeaux. At Barbezieux they stopped to dine, and at La Graulle came upon a bare and desolate heath of vast extent, which gave them a foretaste of the Landes, which they expected shortly to traverse.

At Cubsac, where in our own times there is a suspension-bridge of wondrous size and beauty, they crossed the broad estuary of the Dordogne in a ferry-boat, and had a somewhat perilous passage, the wind being high. However, they got over in safety, and pursued their journey through a fair and fertile region covered with vineyards, and gradually gained an eminence, from the summit of which the wide Garonne, with the proud city of Bordeaux throned on its opposite bank, burst upon their view.

The prospect was magnificent, and held them for some time in admiration. At length they descended the vine-clad slopes of the hill, and tracking a long avenue of fine trees, came to the ferry at La Bastide—there was no bridge then across the Garonne—and immediately embarked.

During their passage across the broad and impetuous river they enjoyed an admirable view of the city, with its old walls, towers, churches, and edifices, chief among which were the cathedral with its twin spires, the Eglise Sainte Croix, Saint Michel with its beautiful detached belfry, Saint Saurin, the old Evêché, and the Hôtel de Ville.

In the port were numerous vessels, for Bordeaux even then was a place of extensive commerce. The travellers landed near one of the ancient city gates, and caused their pack-saddles and horse furniture to be conveyed to an hotel.

Next morning, instead of prosecuting their journey, they spent several hours in inspecting the curiosities of the city, and had just returned from a visit to the port, when the hôtelier entered, and throwing open the door of the salon with as much ceremoniousness as an usher, announced M. le Duc d'Epernon.

The person who entered the room on this announcement was about seventy, but his tall figure was erect, and although his beard and moustaches were grey, his features retained something of the remarkable comeliness which had distinguished them in the days of Henri Trois.

The Duc d'Epernon was attired in a pourpoint and trunk hose of brown quilted satin, with a velvet mantle of the same colour, the latter being ornamented with the order of the Saint Esprit. On his head he wore a black velvet toque, adorned with a red feather and a diamond brooch. Funnel-topped boots, provided with large spurs, completed his costume, and he carried a cravache in his hand.

Immediately on his entrance, Charles and Buckingham arose to meet him, and their appearance and dignity of manner evidently struck him with surprise. While gravely and courteously saluting them, he carefully scanned their features.

"I have to apologise to you for this intrusion, messieurs," he said, with exquisite politeness, "but I will explain the motive of my visit, and then I trust you will excuse it."

"Your visit requires no excuse, M. le Duc," replied Charles, with princely grace. "That a nobleman of such distinction as yourself, one of the brightest ornaments of the courts of Henri Trois and Henri le Grand, should visit persons so obscure as myself and my brother, Tom Smith, is an honour we never could have anticipated, and we cannot fail, therefore, to be highly gratified by your condescension."

" Corbleu! monsieur," cried D'Epernon, bowing and smiling, "unless I am greatly mistaken, there is little condescension on my part. Had I been aware of your rank, rest assured I should not have presented myself in this unceremonious manner, and I must again entreat you to excuse me."

"And I must repeat," returned Charles, " that the honour is entirely on our side. Pray be seated, M. le Duc."

"I have lived too much in courts, monsieur, to be deceived," observed D'Epernon, taking the chair offered him by the prince. " It may please you and your brother to style yourselves the Messieurs Smith, but I do not think I should be far wrong if I gave you the highest titles your country can boast. But to my errand. In me, messieurs, you behold the representative of an epoch, now passed away, when it was customary for the nobility

of France to exercise hospitality towards all strangers. I cannot change my old habits. I have a
château in the neighbourhood of this city, and
chancing to ride over this morning, I accidentally
heard that some English travellers were staying
in this hotel. I therefore came hither to pray you
to be my guests for as long a period as it may
please you to remain with me."

"We would gladly accept your hospitality, M. le
Duc," replied Charles, "but to-morrow we start for
Bayonne and Spain."

"Then I can only express my regret, messieurs,"
replied D'Epernon, rising. "It would have gratified me to entertain you at my château, and to show
you some of the beauties of this country, but I
will not attempt to delay you."

"Stay, M. le Duc," said Buckingham. "With
you there can be no necessity for disguise, and I
will, therefore, inform you that the person whom
you have had the honour of addressing is no other
than Charles, Prince of Wales."

"I felt assured of it," replied D'Epernon, bowing to the ground. "And you, monseigneur, unless I am greatly mistaken, are the Marquis of Buckingham."

"You are right, M. le Duc," said Charles. "But I confide myself to your discretion. I am travelling strictly incognito."

"Your highness may entirely rely on me," returned D'Epernon. "I guess the purpose of your journey to Spain. It is an enterprise worthy of a chivalrous prince like yourself. I trust you may meet with no interruption, and to prevent the chance of your detention at Bayonne, I will furnish you with a letter to the governor of that city, my friend, the Comte de Grammont. I am banished from court, as your highness may possibly be aware, having had the misfortune to make Cardinal Richelieu my enemy; but I have still influence enough for this."

So saying, he sat down at the table, on which writing materials were laid, and traced a few lines on a sheet of paper, which he folded up and respectfully presented to Charles.

"If I can be of any further service, your highness has only to command me," he said.

"You can, indeed, serve me in an important particular, M. le Duc," returned Charles. "I am desirous of sending a despatch to the king my father, and need a trusty courier."

"Your highness need give yourself no further trouble. I will find the man you require. In an hour he shall be ready to start."

"I have yet another favour to ask of you, M. le Duc," said Charles.

"It is granted before asked, prince," replied D'Epernon.

"You may repent your rashness," rejoined Charles, smiling. "However, not to keep you in suspense, I will pray you, if you have no better engagement, to give me your company during the remainder of the day. On some future occasion I shall hope to be your guest."

"I would forego any other engagement to accept the invitation, prince," replied D'Epernon, delighted. "I will but seek out the courier, and then place myself at your highness's disposal during the rest of the day."

"We must talk to you, M. le Duc, of your peerless queen, Anne of Austria, and the lovely princess, Henriette Marie," said Buckingham.

"Have you seen them?" asked D'Epernon, quickly.

"Ay, and danced with them at the Louvre— and without his majesty's knowledge or permission," rejoined Buckingham.

"You surprise me," exclaimed D'Epernon. "I should not have conceived such an adventure possible. But you must regale me with the particulars anon. As I told you, I am a banished man, and know little about the court. But I pity the queen from my heart."

"So do I," sighed Buckingham.

"What think you, prince, of the daughter of

my old master, Henri Quatre?" remarked D'Epernon to Charles. "I have not seen her of late, but she promised to be beautiful, and I hear she is so."

"She is charming," replied Charles, emphatically.

"So charming, that our journey to Madrid had well-nigh come to an end, M. le Duc," observed Buckingham, laughing.

"On her account I would it had," rejoined D'Epernon, smiling. "But I fly to execute your highness's order."

And, with a profound reverence, he quitted the room.

Charles and Buckingham then sat down to prepare their despatches, and gave their "dear dad and gossip" an account of their journey from Paris to Bordeaux, omitting, however, all mention of their adventure in the Forest of Orléans, thinking, with reason, that it might cause his majesty alarm. By the time they had finished, D'Epernon returned, telling them the courier was ready to start, and the despatches were forthwith committed to him.

This done, D'Epernon prayed the prince and his attendants to ride with him to view his château, stating that he had horses at their service, and the proposition being readily agreed to, the party went forth with the duke, and were not a little surprised to find a company of thirty gentlemen attired in the duke's splendid livery, and all well mounted, drawn up before the hotel.

"Are you generally attended by so large an escort as this, M. le Duc?" inquired Charles, smiling.

"Ma foi! prince, this is a very sorry attendance," replied the duke. "During the regency of the queen-mother, I used to go daily to the Louvre with an escort of eight hundred gentlemen."

"So I have heard, M. le Duc," observed Buckingham. "On my return, I will take as large an escort to Whitehall," he thought.

At a sign from D'Epernon, several of his retinue

immediately dismounted, and Charles and his companions being thus provided with horses, the party rode to the duke's château, a vast feudal-looking edifice, situated on an eminence on the left bank of the Garonne, about a couple of leagues from Bordeaux. The terrace commanded a superb view of the noble river that swept past it, as well as of the picturesque city in the distance. The finest wine in the district was grown on the duke's estate, and his guests having tasted it and greatly admired it, D'Epernon insisted upon sending a supply for their consumption at the hotel.

After an hour spent in inspecting the château and its beautiful gardens, the party returned to Bordeaux. An excellent dinner was then served, comprehending most of the delicacies for which Bordeaux is renowned, but its chief merit was the incomparable wine furnished by D'Epernon. More than a dozen flasks were crushed. D'Epernon proved a very agreeable companion, and with pardonable egotism recounted many of the incidents of his eventful life.

"It has been my fate," he said, "to witness the assassination of my two royal masters. I was near Henri Trois when the accursed Dominican, Jacques Clément, plunged a knife into his breast, and I was in the carriage with Henri le Grand when that good king was stabbed by the monster Ravaillac. No monarch was ever more beloved than Henri Quatre, and yet he perished thus. I counsel your highness to be ever on your guard. And you, too, my lord of Buckingham, I would have you take heed. If I am not misinformed, you have bitter enemies amongst the Puritans. Some of those frenzied zealots would deem it a pious act to take your life."

"I have no fear of them," replied Buckingham, with a laugh. "But why do you gaze so hard at me, M. le Duc? Do you read aught in my countenance?"

"You will attain the highest point of your ambition, my lord, but——" And he hesitated.

"Fear not to tell me what you think," said Buckingham.

"You have the same look as my two royal masters," replied D'Epernon. "Be ever on your guard."

This remark produced an impression on Charles, but did not in the slightest degree disturb Buckingham's gaiety. Presently the discourse turned to other topics, and nothing more was thought of the warning.

D'Epernon departed early, and, on taking leave, expressed a hope that he should soon hear of the prince's safe arrival at Madrid, and that all proceeded according to his highness's desire. Accompanied by his escort, the duke then returned to his château.

"Those are two noble-looking personages, and seem to have a great career before them," he thought, as he rode along; "but both will be cut off early"

XVI.

WHAT HAPPENED TO THE TRAVELLERS, AND WHAT THEY BEHELD, AS THEY CROSSED THE GREAT LANDES.

As usual, our travellers started at an early hour in the morning, attended as before by a couple of postilions.

Shortly after quitting the beautiful neighbourhood of Bordeaux, where the plains teemed with plenty, and the heights were covered with vines, they came upon those vast sandy plateaux known as the Great Landes.

No heath they had ever traversed in England appeared so wild and desolate as the apparently interminable waste on which they had now entered. Far as the eye could stretch spread out a vast monotonous plain, flat as the ocean when its waves are still, composed of ash-coloured sand, occasionally rising into little hillocks, covered with heath, stunted broom, and gorse, but without any other sign of vegetation, save that in the extreme distance there were dark lines indicating pine forests. The only discernible road over this dreary waste was the causeway, which the cavalcade was now tracking; and even this was at intervals obliterated by the drifting sand, and could only be recovered by an experienced eye.

The most singular feature of the scene, and that which especially interested our travellers, was the fantastic appearance of the shepherds of the Landes, who looked like inhabitants of some other planet. Before the party had advanced far they noticed a sort of cabin, designated in the language of the country a *parc*, and looking like an enormous mushroom, supported in the centre by the trunk of a tree. Such as it was, this cabin, open to all the winds of heaven, afforded sufficient shelter to the shepherds of the Landes, who lead a nomad life. Near it were three or four herdsmen tending a flock of lean sheep, and a few equally lean cattle, though it was a marvel as to how the animals could obtain sufficient subsistence in that wilderness. The peasants were mounted on stilts, called in their patois *chanques*, which raised them a couple of yards from the ground. Over their shoulders they wore sheepskin cloaks, and berets on their heads, and each was provided with a long pole.

On seeing the travellers, the herdsmen started towards them, moving with gigantic strides, and were soon by the side of the troop. They easily kept up with the horses, even though the latter were going at full speed. After accompanying the cavalcade for half a league, the peasants dropped off, and returned to their flocks.

As our travellers proceeded, and approached the

tracts covered with pines, which flourish vigorously in this sandy soil, and yield a plentiful supply of resin, they found that whatever else the inhospitable region might want, it was by no means destitute of game. Rabbits and hares abounded, a roebuck was now and then descried, and the travellers, catching sight of a wild sow and her marcassins, were half tempted to pursue them. On the plains they saw bustards, in the lakes wild geese, and cranes amid the shallow pools. The marshes were frequented by bitterns, curlews, wild ducks, and coots, and from the pine forests arose clouds of wood-pigeons.

That there were also formidable animals to be encountered, was proved as the party went on. They had just passed a pine forest, and crossed a rude bridge thrown across a stream, the waters of which were black as ink, when they heard loud outcries, and, looking in the direction whence the shouts proceeded, perceived that a flock of sheep had been attacked by a pack of wolves. Three or four shepherds, aided by powerful dogs, were engaged in an unequal conflict with their fierce aggressors; but the wolves were too numerous for them, and had already caused great havoc among the flock. Fortunately, the shepherds were kept by their stilts out of reach of the savage beasts.

Without a moment's hesitation the travellers dashed to the assistance of the shepherds, and, as soon as they were within pistol-shot, fired at the wolves, killing a couple of them, and wounding others. The rest of the pack, displaying their blood-stained fangs, turned fiercely on their assailants, but, ere they could come up, three more dropped by another discharge. Though their numbers were thus thinned, two of the largest and fiercest of the troop attacked Buckingham. From one of these he liberated himself with a stroke of his poniard, and the other was shot by Graham. Another was killed by Charles, and the rest took to flight, pursued by the shepherds and their hounds. This rout being accomplished in a very short space of time, our travellers turned to rejoin the postilions, who prudently awaited their return on the causeway.

Graham, however, had singled out a large wolf, and after a hot pursuit of some two or three hundred yards, succeeded in shooting the ferocious beast. This feat achieved, he dashed across the plain to join the others, who had already regained the causeway. Perceiving the course he was taking, the postilions called out to him, but not understanding the meaning of their cries, and pursuing his career, he was suddenly engulphed in one of those treacherous sand-pits peculiar to the Landes, called in that region *mouvants*. These dangerous quagmires, concealed by a covering of sand supported by aquatic plants and dried on the surface, form traps from which escape is always difficult, and sometimes impossible.

On touching the sandy crust by which the pool was hidden, Graham's horse immediately sank above the shoulder. Luckily the postilions perceived what had occurred, and shouting to him to keep still, hurried to the scene of the disaster, and as soon as they came up, they directed him to dismount cautiously, and then to remain motionless for a few minutes, to allow the sand to settle. This he did; but he had scarcely complied with the injunction when the shepherds came to his assistance, and wading into the pool with their stilts, quickly extricated him from his perilous position. The horse was also dragged out of the quagmire by the exertions of the shepherds, and the travellers were enabled to proceed on their way.

For upwards of four hours they continued their journey through the Landes, changing horses at post-houses, which in several instances were only solitary inns, with large stables attached to them. Everywhere the aspect was the same; vast sandy plains, relieved only by black pine forests, marshes, swamps, pools, and lakes, all of which abounded, as we have mentioned, with wild-fowl of every description. Cabins such as we have already described were frequently to be seen, but the hamlets and villages were composed of miserable habitations. Long before this the travellers had discerned the jagged and snowy peaks of the Pyrenees, and the horizon was now bounded by the long chain of these magnificent mountains.

As the travellers approached a village, which was somewhat larger and better built than any they had as yet beheld in the Landes, they heard the sound of bagpipes, and presently afterwards perceived a band of youths and maidens in holiday attire, decorated with ribands, and carrying bouquets in their hands. While moving along the troop executed a dance to the music of the pipes. Behind them came a large charette, drawn by oxen covered with white housings, and having their horns tied with ribands. In the charette was a pyramid formed of pieces of household furniture, on the top of which sat a middle-aged woman holding a distaff, while round the pile, and standing on the ledges of the cart, were grouped a number of comely damsels.

On inquiry, the travellers learnt that a marriage was about to take place on the following day, and that the bride's furniture was being conveyed in this manner to her future dwelling. The old woman with the distaff was the bride's mother.

In the rear of the charette marched a little procession, headed by the curé of the village and the young couple whom he was so soon about to link together. A large concourse of villagers of both sexes, including many old people and children, made up the procession. All were dressed in their best, and decorated with ribands.

As the travellers moved out of the way to let the jocund train pass by, they were greeted with merry shouts and laughter from the youths and maidens.

No other incident worthy of note happened to the prince and his companions during their ride across the Landes. At Saint Vincent they left the sandy wastes behind them, and entered upon a fertile country.

It was growing dusk as they gained the heights overlooking Bayonne, but sufficient light was left to enable them to discern that strongly fortified town, situated near the junction of the Adour and the Nive.

Descending the hill, they quitted their horses at the faubourg Saint Esprit, and were ferried across both rivers, but were detained at the gates of the town for some time. At last, however, they were permitted to enter, and at once proceeded to an hôtellerie.

XVII.

HOW THE TRAVELLERS WERE BROUGHT BEFORE THE GOVERNOR OF BAYONNE.

THE party had just supped, and, wearied with their long day's journey, were about to retire to rest, when an officer, attended by half a dozen arquebusiers, was shown into their presence, and informed them that he was sent by M. le Comte de Grammont, the governor of Bayonne, to bring them immediately before him.

It being impossible to refuse compliance with

the order, the whole party accompanied the officer, and were taken to the castle, which was situated in the upper part of the town, at no great distance from the hotel. After a brief detention in the guard-chamber, they were led across the inner court to the governor's apartments.

The Comte de Grammont was a haughty-looking personage, of middle age, and he glanced sternly at the travellers as they entered.

"You are Englishmen, messieurs," he said, "on your way to Spain. Is it not so?"

Charles replied in the affirmative, adding, "As we are pressed for time, monseigneur, we desire, with your permission, to start at an early hour to-morrow morning."

"I cannot allow you to do so," replied Grammont, coldly.

"You will perhaps condescend to inform us why we are detained, M. le Comte?" observed Buckingham, haughtily.

"As governor of this city, I have no explanation to render, monsieur," said Grammont. "I shall detain you till I am satisfied on certain points."

"Perhaps we may be able to satisfy you on those points now, monseigneur," remarked Cottington. "We are ready to answer any questions you may please to put to us."

"What is the object of your journey to Spain?" demanded Grammont.

"It cannot be publicly declared, and is not of a nature to interest you, monseigneur," replied Charles.

"Pardieu! I know not that," cried Grammont. "You may be engaged on a secret mission to Spain. You arrive here late in the evening, and propose to start at break of day. I suspect you, messieurs, and shall place you under arrest, and cause your luggage to be searched."

"I protest against such treatment, monseigneur," said Charles, "and I am of opinion that you will exceed your authority if you adopt any such harsh proceeding."

There was something in Charles's look and manner that made the governor hesitate in issuing the order.

"I do not desire to deal harshly with you," he said, "but I must be satisfied. Have you no credentials to exhibit?"

"Only this letter, M. le Comte, from the Duc d'Epernon," replied Charles, producing it.

"A letter from D'Epernon!" exclaimed Grammont.

A marked change came over his countenance as he glanced at it, and respect amounting to deference took the place of his previous haughty manner. He immediately arose, and said:

"I am sorry this letter was not shown me before. All further inquiries are needless, and I have to express my profound regret that you should have been put to so much inconvenience."

"The inconvenience is nothing," returned

Charles. " We are free, I presume, to start on our journey to-morrow morning?"

" At any hour you please," said Grammont. "But it would charm me," he added, " if you could be induced to rest a day at Bayonne. There is much in the town that merits inspection. However, I will not press you further. Reconduct these gentlemen to their hotel," he added to the officer, "and give orders to the guard at the Porte d'Espagne that the whole party be allowed to pass forth when they please to-morrow morning."

" It shall be done, monseigneur," replied the officer, respectfully.

The Comte de Grammont would fain have accompanied the party to the castle gate, but this Charles would not permit.

XVIII.

JACK AND TOM CROSS THE BIDASSOA AND ENTER SPAIN.

BRIGHT and beautiful was the morning, and the sky deep and cloudless, as Charles and his companions quitted Bayonne by the Porte d'Espagne, and passed through the strong fortifications on that side of the town. After riding about a league, the travellers gained a height which commanded a glorious view. On the left was a portion of the vast chain of the Pyrenees, their snowy peaks glittering in the early sunbeams. On the right lay the Bay of Biscay, with its picturesque headlands and bays stretching out as far as Fontarabia. Behind lay Bayonne, and, seen from this point, the city, with its two fine rivers, its ramparts, forts, castle, and churches, presented a very picturesque appearance.

Spain being now in view, Charles's impatience would brook no delay, and, though he could have spent hours in the contemplation of the splendid prospect before him, he quickly gave the word to proceed, and the whole cavalcade was soon moving on at a rapid pace.

Ere long they approached the shores of the sea, and at Bidart, with its charming little bay, entered the Basque country. They next mounted to Gué-tary, then descending again, kept close to the coast, charmed with the views it afforded, till they reached Saint Jean de Luz. Halting merely for a relay of horses at this place, they pursued their course to Urrugne.

On ascending a hill which formed a spur of the lower range of the Pyrenees, they beheld the Bidassoa, the stream dividing France and Spain.

The sight of this river again roused Charles's impatience, and he dashed down the hill to Behobie, a small town on the right bank of the Bidassoa, and the last in France.

Here they were ferried across the river, which at this point boasts two little islands, on one of which the crafty Louis XI. held a conference with Henrique IV. of Castile, and on the other, only eight years prior to the date of our history, the ambassadors of France and Spain met to affiance Philip IV. of Spain to Isabella of France, and Louis XIII. to Anne of Austria. The latter isle, it is needless to say, had a special interest to Charles and Buckingham.

"Heaven be praised, I am at last in Spain!" exclaimed the prince, as he leaped ashore from the boat. "Though I am still far from the Infanta, I am in her own land, and amidst her own people, and the space between us shall speedily be cleared."

The horses and postilions were brought across in another ferry-boat, and as soon as they were landed, the whole party mounted, and galloped off on the left bank of the Bidassoa for Irun, which rose before them on a hill about half a league off. This distance was soon traversed, and Charles and Buckingham, for the first time, entered a Spanish town.

Here all seemed changed, and it was manifest, from the costume and aspect of the inhabitants, and from the appearance of the habitations, with their large balconies and awnings, that the travellers were in a very different country from that which they had left on the other side of the Bidassoa.

The party rode up at once to a posada, and here they were obliged to change the horses they had brought from Urrugne for a relay of mules. The postilions by whom they were attended were much more gaily attired than those of France, and, though small of stature, seemed full of life and activity. Before starting, excellent chocolate was served them by a dark-eyed doncella, whose jetty locks were gathered in a single thick tress behind her back.

Once more they were on their way, and proceeding at a good steady pace, for though the mules resolutely refused to gallop, they trotted faster than the horses. The travellers were now in a picturesque country. Before them, at the extremity of a vast alluvial plain, stood Fontarabia, cresting an eminence overlooking a bay, while inland, on the mountain sides, were groves of mingled oak, chesnut, and walnut.

The cavalcade had passed through Renteria, and were approaching Passage, with its large dock, when they beheld a horseman, whom they took to be a courier, accompanied by a postilion, galloping towards them.

As the person came nearer, however, they perceived that it was young Walsingham Griesley, secretary to the Earl of Bristol, charged, no doubt, with despatches from his master to the King of England.

Griesley could scarcely believe his eyes when he beheld the prince and Buckingham, and they both laughed heartily at the astonishment depicted on his countenance.

"You did not expect to meet us on the way to Madrid, Griesley," cried Charles.

"In truth I did not, your highness," replied the secretary. "I am utterly astounded. But I can guess why you are going thither, and I heartily wish you success. Your highness, however, will find that matters are not so far advanced in regard to the match as you may have been led to expect. I know the purport of the despatches I am conveying to his majesty from my lord of Bristol, and they speak of fresh difficulties which have been thrown in the way by the Conde Olivarez."

"Those difficulties will be easily overcome," cried Buckingham. "Your master allows himself to be duped, Griesley. Things will change when we appear at Madrid."

"I trust they may, my lord," replied the secretary, in a tone that showed he did not anticipate any such result.

"You must ride back with us to Saint Sebastian, Griesley," said Charles. "My lord of Buckingham and myself will add to your despatches to the king. I will also charge you with some messages to his majesty, which can be more easily conveyed by word of mouth than by letter."

"I shall be proud to convey them, my gracious lord," replied Griesley. "I esteem myself singularly fortunate in meeting your highness and my lord marquis, as his majesty cannot fail to be pleased with the good tidings I shall be able to give him of you."

During the ride to Saint Sebastian, Charles and Buckingham had a long conversation with the secretary, and ascertained from him the nature of the difficulties that had arisen; but these they were both disposed to treat very lightly.

On arriving at Saint Sebastian, they put up at the Parador de Postas, and the despatches being prepared, Griesley started once more on his journey.

After an hour's rest, our travellers pursued their way through a beautiful and romantic country to Tolosa, where they passed the night.

XIX.

THE GORGE OF PANCORBO.

NEXT morning the unwearied party started again. Several days of hard travel were still before them ere they could reach their destination, and their powers of endurance were likely to be tested to the utmost by rough roads and obstinate mules that threatened to dislocate their joints. However, they held on gallantly and unflinchingly. Through long valleys—by the side of rushing streams—up precipitous mountains — down steep and dangerous descents—across wide, dreary plains they went, frequently encountering bands of muleteers armed with trabucos, and conducting strings of gaily-caparisoned mules laden with heavy pack-saddles, but though hearing much of robbers, and occasionally meeting suspicious-looking personages in the mountain passes, they had hitherto escaped attack.

On the evening of the third day after quitting Bayonne they reached Miranda de Ebro, where they rested for the night, and proceeding next morning through the valley of the Oroncillo, they entered the Gorge of Pancorbo, a gloomy ravine hemmed in on either side by mountains, and en-closed by rugged rocks, between which rushes the Oroncillo.

While the travellers were threading this savage pass, and gazing at the tremendous precipices that threatened to topple on their heads, they were startled by the report of fire-arms, evidently pro-ceeding from the lower part of the gorge, which was concealed from view by a huge projecting rock.

"What mean those shots?" cried Graham, who was somewhat ahead of the party.

"Ladrones, señor caballero!" returned one of the postilions, crossing himself. "Saints preserve us, they are plundering some travellers, perhaps murdering them!"

Without a word more, Graham applied spurs to his mule, and rode on as fast as he could.

On passing the rock, which screened the lower part of the ravine from view, he beheld a spectacle that roused him to still greater exertion. About two hundred yards lower down, where the gorge was somewhat wider, though the rocks were still precipitous, the torrent was crossed by a picturesque wooden bridge, close beside which, on the opposite side of the stream, was a large travelling-carriage, surrounded by banditti, who were now actively engaged in rifling it of its contents.

The postilion and an old attendant had been shot, probably at the time when the report of fire-arms reached the ears of our travellers, and their bodies were lying on the ground near the carriage. The traces had been cut, and the mules removed to a little distance from the vehicle.

On the other side of the carriage, guarded by a couple of brigands, stood an old hidalgo, for such his appearance and attire proclaimed him. He had been wounded in the attack, and was binding a handkerchief round his arm. Graham's attention, however, was diverted from the hidalgo by loud shrieks from the bridge. Two ladies, who it appeared had escaped from the clutches of the brigands, and were flying across the bridge, had just been recaptured, and now made the rocks ring with their screams. One of them, who struggled violently with her captor, was young, beautiful, and richly dressed, and was, no doubt, the hidalgo's daughter. The other, who was much older, might be her dueña. As Graham hurried on to the rescue of the affrighted ladies, both bandits discharged their pistols at him, but they were too much embarrassed by their captives to take good aim. Graham replied with better effect. Both robbers were hit by his shots. One of them rolled into the torrent, and the other released his prey and fled. Thus liberated, the ladies flew towards their preserver, and met him just as he reached the foot of the bridge. The younger of the two, who was half wild with terror, with her dishevelled locks hanging about her shoulders, called out piteously,

"My father! my dear father! save him, señor! It is the Conde de Saldana."

"Your father shall soon be set free, señorita. My friends are at hand," said Graham, pointing to the advancing troop.

"Calm yourself, Doña Casilda," cried the dueña; "calm yourself, my child. The saints on whom we called for aid have brought this noble caballero to deliver us from a fate worse than death."

"Do not stay here, señorita," cried Graham. "You are exposed to danger. Take shelter behind yon rock. I will soon bring your father to you."

"Thanks! oh thanks, señor," exclaimed Doña Casilda, with a grateful glance at her preserver. And, accompanied by the dueña, she flew to the place of refuge which had been pointed out to her.

At the same moment the cavalcade came up.

Meantime, the brigands, alarmed by the appearance of such a force as the travellers presented, had seized their firelocks, and, rushing towards the bridge, seemed determined to prevent the cavalcade from crossing it. Fearing that mischief might occur to the prince, Graham besought him to hold back, but Charles would not be stayed, and calling to the others to follow him, prepared at all hazards to drive the robbers from the bridge.

Fortunately at this moment shouts were heard farther down in the gorge, and a small detachment of musketeers was seen hurrying to the scene of action. At this sight, finding they would soon be outnumbered, and would also be attacked in rear and front, the brigands turned and fled, quickly disappearing among the rocks. So precipitate was their flight, that they were unable to take any of the booty with them.

Two of the band, however, aided by a black-visaged ruffian, who appeared from his air of command to be the captain, endeavoured to carry off the Conde de Saldana, probably hoping to obtain a large sum for his ransom. Seizing the old hidalgo by the arms, they tried to drag him off, while the captain, holding a poniard to his breast, threatened, with terrible oaths, to stab him to the heart if he resisted.

In this manner they succeeded in dragging him among the rocks, and might have got clear off with their prey, if Graham had not come to his assistance. Firing at the robber chief, and wounding the villain, Graham sprang from his mule and bounded up the rocks. The robbers did not await his approach, but, releasing the Conde de Saldana, made good their retreat. Graham did not attempt to pursue them, neither did he bestow any thought on their leader, who was lying on a shelf of rock, but assisted the old hidalgo to descend.

By this time Charles and his companions had come up, and a few moments later the musketeers arrived on the spot, and after securing the wounded captain, and binding him hand and foot, they scrambled up the rocks in search of the rest of the band.

It appeared that these musketeers had just arrived at the village of Pancorbo, which lay at the end of the gorge, about a quarter of a league off, when the sound of fire-arms had brought them to the scene of attack.

As may well be supposed, the old hidalgo's first inquiries were for his daughter, and he was not kept long in suspense in regard to her safety. Impelled by curiosity, which was stronger than their fears, Doña Casilda and her dueña ventured from their place of refuge, and finding that the robbers had been driven off, they hurried across the bridge, and arrived at the spot where the carriage was left at the precise moment that the Conde de Saldana was brought there by Graham.

Uttering a cry of delight, Doña Casilda threw herself upon her father's neck, while the old hidalgo, in his delight at beholding her, forgot his wound and all that had befallen him. Not to interrupt their meeting, Charles and his attendants moved away to a short distance.

"How have you been preserved, my child?" cried the old hidalgo, as he recovered from his emotion.

"Señora Engracia and myself were rescued by this gentleman," replied Doña Casilda, pointing to Graham.

"He also was my deliverer," said the Conde de Saldana. "Señor," he added to Graham, "may I ask to whom we are thus greatly indebted."

"I am Sir Richard Graham, an English gentleman, Señor Conde, and am on my way to Madrid," replied the young man.

"You have done me an incalculable service, Sir

Richard," said the old hidalgo. "I rejoice to learn that you are travelling to Madrid. You will find a home, if you please, at the Casa Saldana. I will also introduce you to the court of our young king, Felipe IV. My daughter and myself are on our way to Madrid, and were posting from Miranda to Burgos when this attack occurred. Heaven be praised it is no worse!"

"But you are wounded, father!" cried Doña Casilda.

"It is but a trifling hurt," replied the hidalgo. "I will get it dressed by the barber-chirurgeon at Pancorbo. These are your friends, Sir Richard?" he added, as Charles and Buckingham approached.

"Friends and compatriots," replied Graham.

The old hidalgo courteously saluted them, and thanked them warmly for the assistance they had rendered him. Though evidently much struck by the distinguished appearance of the prince and Buckingham, he forbore to inquire their names. He afterwards, however, told his daughter that he was confident they were persons of the highest rank.

The exertions of the whole party were now directed towards enabling the Conde de Saldana and his daughter to proceed on their journey. Luckily, the mules were uninjured, and they were speedily harnessed to the carriage by ropes. All the articles scattered about by the brigands were quickly collected together and replaced in the coffers, and everything being rearranged as well as circumstances permitted, the old hidalgo, with his daughter and the dueña, once more took their seats in the carriage. The place of the unlucky driver who had been shot by the brigands was supplied by one of the postilions in attendance upon our travellers, and all being settled at last, the whole party proceeded to Pancorbo—Charles and his companions forming an escort to the carriage.

At Pancorbo, the Conde de Saldana alighted to have his wound dressed, and here our travellers took leave of him and his daughter, and pursued their journey to Burgos.

"We shall hope to see you on our arrival at Madrid, Don Ricardo," said Doña Casilda, as she bade adieu to Graham.

"I shall not fail to present myself, señorita," he replied. "But perhaps you may have forgotten me by that time."

"I am not so ungrateful," she said, fixing her magnificent black eyes somewhat reproachfully upon him. "Hasta la vista, señor!"

"Adios, señorita!"

XX.

HOW SIR RICHARD GRAHAM MET WITH AN ADVENTURE IN THE CATHEDRAL OF BURGOS.

JUST at sunset the travellers approached Burgos. On quitting Pancorbo they had made the best of their way across broad plains, over steep and barren mountains, and through narrow valleys, obtaining fresh relays of mules at Briviesca, Rodilla, and Quintanapalla. At eventide, as we have said, they drew near the old capital of Old Castile.

From its associations with the renowned Cid Campéador, Burgos possessed strong interest for our romantic and chivalrous prince, and it was not without emotion that he first caught sight of the twin spires of its incomparable cathedral.

Ere long, as he gained an eminence, the whole of the ancient and picturesque city rose before him—its old walls, its gates, its proud castle, its countless towers and steeples brought out in black relief against the glowing sky.

Above all these structures, like a giant amid a host of pigmies, domineered the gigantic cathedral. All the upper part of the fabric—the mighty roof, the noble central tower with its pinnacles, and the two exquisitely crocketed spires, of which we have just spoken, each springing to a height of three hundred feet—could now be clearly discerned.

Between the travellers and Burgos lay the Vega, a fair and fertile plain, richly wooded in the part adjacent to the city, and watered by the river Arlanzon, now crimsoned by the setting sun. Crowning a hill about half a league from the eminence on which the prince had halted to survey the scene, stood the Cartuja de Miraflores, a magnificent convent, built in the fifteenth century, in the purest Gothic style, and which had served as a mausoleum for the old monarchs of Castile.

Charles remained rapt in contemplation of this beautiful prospect, until the shades of night, which came on too quickly, shrouded it from his view. Even in the gloom he could distinguish the giant mass of the cathedral, and the still shining Arlanzon flowing through the wooded Vega.

After traversing a bridge across the river, and passing through a lofty gateway, the cavalcade entered the city, and proceeded along several streets, the houses of which seemed of great antiquity, many of them being decorated with stone escutcheons, and curiously painted.

These streets were only lighted by lanterns hung in front of the shops, or by candles burning before some holy image. But there were plenty of people abroad—dames and damsels draped in mantillas, caballeros muffled in black cloaks, monks, priests, alguacils, officers of the Inquisition, barbers, soldiers, vagabond boys, and beggars without number. In the aspect and deportment of these people— beggars and boys included—the proud Castilian character was displayed. All had a grave, haughty air, and marched like hidalgos. Pride and poverty went hand in hand. A ragged cloak seemed to be accounted no disgrace to its wearer—at least, he did not appear ashamed of it. In the balconies of many of the houses parties of young persons were assembled, and the tinkling of guitars was frequently heard.

The streets being narrow, and, moreover, encumbered by vehicles of various kinds and strings of mules, the progress of the cavalcade was necessarily slow. At last they issued into a large plaza, on one side of which, hemmed in by inferior buildings, stood the cathedral, and thither, as soon as they had secured rooms at the parador, where they alighted, Charles and Buckingham immediately repaired, fortunately arriving in time to witness the solemnisation of evening mass.

Prepared as they were for a wondrous spectacle, the grand coup d'œil offered by the interior of the cathedral far surpassed any expectations they had formed of it, and struck them with reverential awe. Emerging from one of the aisles into the mighty nave, they stood still for a short time to contemplate the sublime picture. A large portion of the fane was plunged in gloom, but this obscurity added to the effect of such parts as could be distinguished. The twinkling tapers attached to the long line of pillars on either side, though only serving to make darkness visible in the aisles, cast sufficient light on the nave to disclose the numerous figures kneeling on the pavement. These devotees were for the most part women, who, even while reciting their prayers, never ceased to agitate their fans. All, without exception, wore mantillas, and were attired in black. Scattered amongst them were a few men in varied and picturesque costumes.

The grand altar at which the priests were officiating was a blaze of light, and the splendour of this part of the scene was heightened by the surrounding gloom. The prince and Buckingham might have regretted that so many architectural beauties—so many exquisite sculptures and paintings—were hidden from their view; that the glories of the gorgeous painted windows were not called forth by external light, and the charming perspectives formed by the triple rows of pillars in the aisles were only imperfectly revealed; but, such as it was, the picture was perfect of its kind, and delighted them as much as if every detail had been fully revealed.

Moving slowly down the nave, ever and anon glancing between the pillars of the aisles at some lovely but dimly-seen chapel, or pausing to gaze at a painting or statue that attracted their attention, the prince and his companion approached the choir, where the light afforded by the great altar-candles was sufficiently strong to enable them to discern the marvellous workmanship of the stalls,

the superb retablo, with its spiral pillars and con-
summately beautiful statues, and overhead the glorious dome, storied with the arms of kings and
archbishops—a dome which Philip II. pronounced
to be so beautiful, "that it seemed the work of
angels rather than the production of men."

Having examined all these marvels, so far as was
practicable under the circumstances — the sacred
rites were then being performed at the high altar
—the prince and Buckingham glided noiselessly
away, and proceeded to the grand Gothic chapel,
called the Capilla del Condestable — in itself a
church — where they beheld a marvellous altar-
screen and several tombs of extraordinary beauty
—chief among the latter being the tomb of Don
Pedro Hernandez de Velasco, constable of Castile,
and founder of the chapel. They were next taken
by a sacristan, who, seeing they were strangers,
volunteered to act as their cicerone, to the chapter-
house, where they saw, fastened against the wall,
an old wooden coffer of great size, and strengthened

by bands of iron, described by their conductor as "the Chest of the Cid."

The legend connected with this singular coffer was recounted to them by the sacristan, and was to the effect that the Cid, being in want of money, filled the chest with old armour, and then taking it to a wealthy Hebrew, represented to him that its contents were vessels of silver and gold, and demanded six hundred marks on the deposit, stipulating at the same time that the chest should not be opened till the loan was repaid. The Jew, who was either more credulous and confiding than the generality of his tribe, or had a profound respect for the Cid, accepted the conditions, and counted out the money. Whether the Cid performed his part of the engagement the sacristan could not tell, but he held the stratagem not only to be perfectly justifiable, but praiseworthy. He would have told them other stories of the renowned Gothic warrior, whose name is the boast of Burgos, but they had heard enough, and returned to the body of the cathedral.

Vespers were just over, the great altar-candles were already extinguished, and the chanters and sub-chanters were closing the magnificent gilt iron gates of the choir. Still some light was afforded by the tapers, which were left burning before the shrines and against the ranges of columns on either side of the nave. A few devotees still lingered, as if resolved to remain to the latest moment.

Reluctant to quit the sacred fabric, with the wondrous beauty of which they were quite smitten, Charles and Buckingham were standing near the centre of the nave, gazing around, when they were joined by Graham.

"You are late, Dick," said Buckingham, in a low tone to him. "Mass is over."

"I know it. I have been here for some time— quite long enough to meet with an adventure," replied the other.

"An amorous adventure, of course," remarked Buckingham.

"Your lordship shall hear. I was standing near the last pillar of yonder aisle, when a lady, while passing hastily by me, slipped a billet into my hands."

"Bah! she mistook you for her lover."

"Very likely," replied Graham. "But, at all events, here is the commencement of an adventure, if I choose to pursue it. I ought to tell your lordship that I had previously seen the lady kneeling before a statue of the Virgin in the Capilla de Santa Ana, and though her features were partly concealed by her envious mantilla, I could make out that she had an adorable countenance, and superb black eyes."

"Was she alone?" inquired Buckingham.

"An elderly dame was with her, whom I took to be her dueña," replied Graham.

"How is the billet addressed?" asked Buckingham.

"It bears no superscription, and I have not yet opened it," returned Graham.

While this conversation took place, two tall cavaliers, wrapped in black cloaks, issued from the aisle on the left, and stationed themselves at a little distance from the party, on whom they were evidently keeping watch.

Their manner quickly attracted Buckingham's attention, and he said to Graham,

"By my faith, Dick, your adventure is likely to have an awkward termination. I'll be sworn that one of those scowling cavaliers, who look as if they would willingly cut your throat, is the lover of the lady from whom you received the billet. Give it him, and explain how you got it."

"Not I—unless he asks for it civilly," replied Graham.

"Well, do as you please. If you have to fight, I will stand by you. The prince is about to depart. Keep near us."

No part of the foregoing discourse had reached

the ear of Charles, neither had he remarked the two cavaliers, who now followed them like shadows.

As the party passed out by a side portal, Buckingham observed to the prince,

"I must pray your highness to return to the parador alone. Graham and I have a word to say to yonder cavaliers."

"Who are they?" demanded Charles, noticing the two mysterious-looking personages for the first time.

"I know no more than your highness; but they have had the impertinence to follow us."

"Do not provoke a quarrel, Geordie," said the prince.

"Rest easy," replied Buckingham. "I have no such design. We will rejoin your highness very shortly."

Satisfied with this assurance, Charles quitted his attendants, and proceeded across the plaza towards the parador.

No sooner was he gone than the two cavaliers, who were standing at a little distance watching them, came up, and one of them, in accents of constrained courtesy, said to Graham,

" You have received a billet from a lady, señor. I must beg you to give it me, or I shall be forced to take it from you."

" Aha! you must be jesting, señor," rejoined Graham. " I value the billet too highly to surrender it."

" Voto á Dios! I *will* have it!" cried the other, no longer able to contain himself. " It was given to you by mistake, señor. It was intended for me."

" So you tell me, señor," rejoined Graham.

"I swear to you I speak the truth. I am a Castilian noble, señor, and my word has never yet been doubted."

" And I am an English gentleman, señor, and never yet brooked an affront," rejoined Graham. "I will not part with the letter unless you can make good your vaunt, and take it from me."

"Básta, señor!" said the cavalier. "Be pleased to follow me to a more retired spot."

"This is a very foolish affair, Dick," observed Buckingham, "and if any harm should come of it, the prince will blame me. I cannot allow it to proceed."

"But I cannot now retreat with honour, my lord," rejoined Graham.

"I am waiting for you, señor," cried the cavalier, in a taunting tone.

"Before we consent to follow you, señor, we must know whither you would take us," interposed Buckingham.

"The place is close by, señor," returned the cavalier who had not hitherto spoken. "A couple of minutes will suffice to bring you to it."

"So far good," observed Buckingham. "We will give you ten minutes to adjust the affair."

"Five will suffice," cried the first cavalier, impatiently. "While we have been talking here the matter might have been settled."

"Vamos, señores, vamos!" rejoined Buckingham, haughtily.

END OF VOL. I.

LONDON:
PRINTED BY C. WHITING, BEAUFORT HOUSE, STRAND.

'THE CADMUS BOOK SHOP